# BLACK
# GOLD

A NOVEL

christine racheal

# dedication

For the hero in every woman whose story remains untold,
for those with unspoken contributions to *her*story, and for
all Black Gold who will not be ignored.

# preface

Years ago, while I perused various news articles, I stumbled across a story in *The Florida Times Union* about a community that would be demolished in my native Jacksonville, Florida. It had become decrepit and was no longer thriving. It stunned me that this community was located near the neighborhood where I spent most of my childhood—a place where loved ones and friends still reside.

As I continued to read, the periodical described the woman who inspired the development of that community, and it included a brief highlight of her life. I was hooked to the story of Princess Laura Kofi who had come to America to liberate blacks in the 1920s. With an origin in Accra, an economic center and capital of the country we now know as Ghana, her purpose was to inspire the descendants of the stolen people to unify, to build, to establish trade, and to return to their native land. And like Marcus Garvey, whose legacy is well known in the US, and who graces numerous history books taught in the American classroom, she desired a great exodus of struggling blacks—one that would result in the restoration of identity and total liberty, one that had not been accessible in America then, or now.

How could I not have known? Was it because her time in America stretched a mere eighteen months, or because she has no living relatives in this land to shed light on her contribution to black American history, or was it because she was a woman like others whose community impact frequently went overlooked and overshadowed by those of men? I never learned the answer, but I was determined to honor her life by creating an opportunity for her story to be heard and shared.

The link to the news article remained open in my

phone's browser for nearly a year until the day I decided to look a little further. I spent weeks researching the life of Laura Kofi and her involvement with the UNIA (Universal Negro Improvement Association) under the leadership of Marcus Garvey, and how her story was connected to a place I had called home my entire life. I reflected on how her contribution to black society escaped traditional history books and common tales within the black community, yet there was very little room for me to be completely appalled once I considered the fact that only recently have more truths of our ancestors' contributions to American history been unearthed—and may fail to ever become common knowledge. The life of a *woman* whose light drew thousands to God, and then inspired them to build and unite to create change, would continue to evade us. Only few took the chance to present her story and her cause to the masses.

Furthermore, American society for blacks has never presented a level playing field. The hardships are beyond apparent. With poverty and a consistent lack of educational resources in black communities, it is impossible to ignore that there is more work to be done for equal access and impartial treatment. Yet, the rise of social media influence coupled with a lack of knowledge and unity within the community, a heavy shadow is cast over the important issues that continue to plague us. What you will notice as you read this novel is that the causes Laura Kofi stood for, and the lack of unity that she spoke against in the 1920s, have not since met full resolve. While we acknowledge and honor our fallen (s)heroes, we must think of how they would address current socioeconomic issues and injustices, and then act in a way that would lead to change. To truly pay homage to these brave individuals, we must consistently measure the progress of what each of them fought for, and the *current* degree of oppression they fought against, to recognize that there is still work to be done.

And finally, the title of this novel was inspired by a poem that I penned in college—March 30, 2007 to be exact.

I had walked past a flyer in Florida State University's Student Union, and it announced that there would be a speaker in one of the large lecture halls the following evening. Without prior knowledge of the speaker, I decided to attend. In all his glory, Amiri Baraka, poet laureate and revolutionary, set the room on fire. It is impossible to describe what it felt like to be engulfed in his passionate words, so I went back to my apartment that evening, and wrote the following poem, entitled "To Amiri Baraka: I Am Black".

*You* make me proud
proud to have been born into
flesh rooted in the suffrage
of my ancestors
with aching backs and bleeding fingers
weeding their master's backyards
in burning red clay of Georgia
as their own seeds were ripped
from their womb
to help birth a nation
they don't get credit for.

To be called an African American
is understated.
Going beyond bar-coding
the Negro slave and stripping
man of his own identity.
For the names of Africa had significance
that surpassed the tyrant's vision of our future.
Then Fahim becomes Frank,
Jabari becomes James,
from Chaniya, meaning rich, to Shannon
from Malia, meaning queen, to Martha
from the African slave to the African *American*—slave.
A name that serves no justice has no right to be given.
A name that continues to oppress,

making second-class citizenship acceptable
as the proper place for black faces.

America, which allowed the Body of Liberties in 1641
to make bondage legal
is disassociated from the ethnicity
that I proudly proclaim to have been born.
Slavery is not dead! Slavery is not dead!
but has metamorphosed into
other forms of exploitation and domination
in which we are *still* at the very bottom
From the coast of Jamestown in 1619 to
the disappointments of corporate America in 2007,
we are still working to earn our freedom.

I am the seed of Kenya and Uganda,
the niece of Nigeria and Ghana,
cousin to Guinea, Liberia, and Gambia,
for I am rooted in a land never called home
but I am black, as black as what many call the second
half of the day,
that without it, life would be nonexistent.
I am black, as black as oil in its natural state
worthy of bloodshed in deserts because
my being can become the fertilizer that flowers
the seeds and become the plants that feed you
that energy-rich fuel that can carry you
and makes the idea of human flight possible.
I am beyond what the Royal African Company of 1672
declared to be "black gold",
valuable for my strength and knowledge
high in demand and expressively profitable.
I am black, as black as the ink from my pen
that spread a message and relieved many
of a writer's block before they knew they could write,
the black ink that pours from the soul,
streaming from the black blood

pumping through my arteries
and allowing me to breathe, allowing me to be black,
allowing me to be proud.

Identity, the core of who we are, is something many of us fail to fully grasp. Others go on quests to understand their design and purpose—and then another to accept what is revealed. What we know of Laura Kofi is that she was a woman who never wavered in what she desired for blacks in America. I was fascinated by her life, but her uncovered history was limited to her cause—her "honorable mission," if you will. So, *Black Gold* is a snippet of the life of this powerful woman, and is interwoven with the character, pitfalls, relationships, and sentiments of the woman I imagined her to be. This is *my* version of the life of Princess Laura Kofi.

# CHAPTER
# ONE

Like metal to a magnet, she was drawn to America—rough, hard—and with failed resistance. The call had come as apparently as each breath, and the lure was far from appealing, yet Laura's yellow scarf billowed in the salty, warm air as land appeared on the horizon. Her eyes were sharp and focused; her countenance was stern and alluring. Silken mocha, her skin radiated the inner glow of the sun at daybreak. She exhaled in acceptance of what was ahead. Amongst thousands of new immigrants, very few of color, her delicate hands rattled along the ship's railing as her breath became increasingly shallow. The pressure of the unknown possessed her, and when she realized it, she closed her eyes, breathed deeply again, and was released.

The itinerary read: SEPTEMBER 1926. Laura folded it into a long, narrow rectangle and gently placed it into her bag as the boat's anchor cut through the river beneath them. She lifted her head, and she and America became quickly acquainted. She learned her proper place—separate from others. A sign, "NEGROES EXIT LEFT" was displayed on the dock. For a moment, she glanced at those who stood nearby and were of a fairer complexion, and she was reminded that she was longer amongst the majority; it had escaped her as she journeyed from a land where black was deeply rooted in the soil of all existence, to a land where black was merely the stain of a once useable tool—a resource long abandoned and undervalued.

Beyond the sign was a middle-aged black man. He anxiously waited, and fidgeted with his hands. He was tall in stature, quite dark, and would occasionally pivot slightly from one foot to the other. Adrenaline had directed his movements. Neatly dressed in dark pants and a white collared shirt, he lifted his hands near his brow to shield his eyes from the sun as he looked out over the water to the massive ship.

The very few minorities gathered among "others" who had yet to grasp the depth of their privilege—devoid of color—and they all exited the ship. As Laura took her first step onto the dock, the man in wait of her gently grabbed her small suitcase, stamped with evidence of her European travels.

"Missionary?"

"What gave it away?" Laura asked in a flowery African dialect. She removed the scarf from her head, and revealed a loosely pinned bun of coarse hair; her coils were intricately combed and laid into place.

"The aura of a woman on a mission." He took her by the arm. "Even more, it's the sound of Africa in your voice."

Laura nodded pleasantly, and when the two were far enough from water, he released her.

"God be pleased," she said with a faint smirk and slightly bowed her head.

"How was the journey down from Canada?" he asked.

"Swifter than the voyage from Accra weeks ago. So, it would be meaningless to complain."

"I thought you'd be traveling with others. Being a woman, out here alone on such a voyage, and of noble blood too. I expected," he paused, "more." He failed to mention her physical attributes—the slight pucker of her full lips, her curves, noticeable even with her modestly long skirt and fully buttoned blouse—a beauty that required no adornment of any kind, but like his previous comments, that would also be irrelevant.

Laura removed her gloves as she spoke, "It may not look like much, but I have all I need."

The driver sensed that he must have insulted her and lowered his head regretfully. "You're mistaken. Forgive me." He stumbled over his words, "I-I-I just thought you'd be travelling with others. We've made accommodations f-f-for several guests in the apartment."

"That's fine. And thank you, but I only need room for one. I was told to travel lightly, so I tried to carry nothing weightier than the Word." The two continued to walk together towards the car.

"Well, ma'am, modesty is a great quality."

"I believe it depends on what you're modest about."

Once they reached the car, the driver opened the passenger door for Laura to climb in before he took his position behind the wheel and pulled away.

The driver was cautious with his words—unfamiliar with how to carry on conversation with someone of Laura's nobility and culture, and so he settled for silence. Laura noticed the deformity of his hand as he gripped the steering wheel, and grew curious, but her sensitive nature prevented her from questioning him directly. She feared she would appear rude or offend him.

"You never told me your name, sir."

"Michael. My daddy gave it to me." He pondered. "He said it was *his* daddy's name—and he died in the war. And Daddy not much good these days either. Old age set in, and it ain't much help we can find for him."

"And your mother?"

"Mama died years ago. I was still a boy. Ten." He checked his surroundings as he turned a corner where several pedestrians lingered in the dirt roadway. "She was a good woman, but the good Lord knows better than us. Died in a fire one afternoon. I'll never forget it. Ole youngsters belonging to the family she and my daddy worked for was always into things. Those boys kept up with all kinds of mischief." Laura's eyes centered on the storyteller.

He continued, "Set fire to the shed right near our house one morning—just playing around. Wind caught hold of it. I could hear my mama's screams from behind the big house. Without even thinking, I ran as fast as I could to help her, knowing my daddy was away working crops." He wiped his brow with the back of his hand. "It was so hot. I thought I could take it for just long enough to get her out, but I could only get as much as a part of my arm in before missus pulled me back out. It burned like hell." He lifted his hand and examined the damage. "By that time, I didn't hear her screaming anymore."

Laura had her answer.

"And what happened with the boys?"

"Only that they couldn't go out to play for a while, but nothing other than that," he chuckled, appalled by his truth. "The family buried my mama not too far from the property. There wasn't much of a fuss to be made. Daddy was already having it bad finding work with his back always troubling him—and to care for us himself, he couldn't afford to say or do much at all. He knew in his heart there wasn't any ill-will. Just sheer carelessness."

Silence swept through the vehicle, and the two rode slowly and quietly through dust-riddled areas—land cleared to make room for grander buildings and factories, the promise of industry. With the dinner hour quickly approaching, they proceeded through a community where foot traffic had become heavy.

With childlike excitement, Laura peered through the window as she traveled a neighborhood adorned with beautifully crafted homes. Gray smoke seeped from their chimneys; quiet, solid steps led to their front doors; wooden gate posts imprisoned the leveled grass—a palace or sanctuary. The spotless front window of one home displayed a white, young mother who spoon-fed her infant at the dining room table. On the sidewalks, children played joyfully—running, jumping, singing.

Storefront windows enticed her to plead for a stop, but the driver's uncomfortable posture—shoulders raised, both hands firmly on the steering wheel—silenced her request. The aroma of freshly baked bread and pie loomed around her, and she inhaled its sweetness. The community's white inhabitants, all of its inhabitants, would greet each other, and then stand near street corners to converse for a while before they parted ways.

And like the flick of a switch, there was dust on all sides. Laura's expression dimmed the moment she crossed the railroad tracks, a tangible barrier that made the racial divide as distinctive as night is from day. The road, once smooth and easy to travel, became rocky and discordant. Laura grasped the vehicle's door with her hand and held it tightly. The ash-covered buildings were riddled with broken windows. Several black men and women rested lazily on the stoops of apartment buildings. An elderly gentleman puffed on a cigarette that never touched his hands. The ash fell silently to his lap; he did not budge—more people would swat a roaming fly faster than he responded to the sting of embers from his cigarette. His lips tightened around it as he inhaled before he loosened them again to release the smoke; his eyes followed every movement on the road, but nothing more. A toddling girl stood barefoot and pulled her ragdoll from the hole where she had buried it.

Near sunset, the car came to a full stop in front of an apartment building set between mediocrity and poverty. Laura graciously took in her surroundings as the driver exited the car. He walked over to open the door before he pulled her luggage from the rear.

He spoke. "I-I know it's not much to look at from out here, but we set you up real nice inside."

"Why is it so—different?" Laura could not resist. Her curiosity caused the words to linger at the very edge of her tongue.

He asked, puzzled, "In what way?"

Laura pointed in the direction of the vibrant, white neighborhood. "The road leading here was lined with trees and children playing. And here—it's so cold, bare."

"Well, Ms. Laura, that there is Greenbriar. That's for whites only. It stretches about five miles east of here, and we can go and shop for what we need, but we don't stay much longer than necessary. They aren't too fond of Negro folks around there."

"But they're quite fond of Negro money, I see." Laura tightened the button on her blouse as the crisp, evening air caused her to shiver.

"How is it over there—you know—in Africa? Are houses like these over there?"

"In some parts, you'd see dwellings such as these, but the faces you'll see won't appear so miserable. The people take pride in their community—even the ones that are unsanitary and abandoned by whites who took our best homes, and created barriers, like the ones you have here, between us and them."

"So, blacks are separated from whites in Africa too?"

"We were. Yellow fever and malaria—their excuse for the divide. We knew it wasn't so. The fight never ceased— they took our homes while they collected our taxes, and did all they could to make us inferior, but we are a resilient people."

"Folks around here have been through so much that most of them have little motivation to do much else but survive the cold and stay out of white folks' way."

"That doesn't seem hard."

"It's harder than you think." He nudged her arm. "I'll

show you inside."

He led Laura up the stoop and into an upstairs apartment. The interior was clean, and everything had its place, although it was sparsely furnished. There was a single burgundy sofa pushed against a wall, a simple coffee table sat before it, and an additional table rested beneath the windows on the far side of the room. The scent of lemon sliced the air and was incredibly refreshing. The driver placed her bag off the entryway and pointed as he instructed.

"There you have the kitchen. And to the right are two bedrooms. A linen closet's down the hall. But there isn't much food. Coming from Africa and all, we didn't know what to get you."

Laura draped her scarf over the back of the sofa and was lured to a window, the eyes of her new place of rest.

"Thank you. It will do just fine."

"Sure you don't need anything?"

She placed her hand on a radio nestled on the table near the window, and pressed a button to turn it on. She looked to the driver. "Thank you," she dismissed him. He backed out of the doorway and closed the door shut. Laura watched him from the window; he stepped lightly to his car as the burden of hospitality had been lifted. When he was out of sight, she increased the volume of the radio and watched young people scurry home before they lost the dim glow of the sky.

An animated, fast-talking, masculine voice sprawled over the airwaves. "Today, Marcus Garvey, the founder of the Universal Negro Improvement Association, and a man J. Edgar Hoover characterized as 'a notorious Negro agitator' was convicted of mail fraud and having numerous financial gaps in accounting while under investigation. This leader of a reported 4 million members is set to serve 5 years in prison. You've tuned in to Detroit's finest broadcast hour. We will be back in a moment."

Laura breathed in deeply, and then parted her lips to

release the remnants of worry she carried to America with her, and whispered, "Do with me what You will, Lord."

After a chilling bath, a towel-wrapped Laura emerged with dewy skin that glistened in the poorly lit room. She turned on the water at the faucet, which protested in her attempt to rinse the stained sink. She paused, and stared boldly into the mirror. Her look softened as she mustered a smile and appeared to practice her facial expressions—she squinted her eyes, raised her eyebrows, twitched her nose, smiled subtly.

"I am—," she proclaimed to an invisible audience but, displeased with her tone, she stopped to clear her throat. "I am a representative—." She shifted her pitch, "I am a representative of the Gold Coast." Laura's attitude became more serious, "The Gold Coast." She shook her head, embarrassed by her private behavior.

A streak of moonlight ran parallel to her bed, and before she laid down for rest, she kneeled before the God who called her to journey by sea to a land of unfamiliar faces, with unfamiliar customs, but with similar prejudices. She needed help for the journey, and she sought it in the solitude of the midnight hour.

She did not speak. She listened for a time that passed with the swiftness of a caterpillar clinging tightly to a leaf. She listened with her heart, certain that answers had already been breathed into the atmosphere, and then laid herself down with a peace that overflowed into her restful sleep.

# CHAPTER
# TWO

With morning came the melodic chirps of birds—a ballad for sunrise, but it was interrupted by a screech that echoed from the kitchen. Laura's eyes widened as she found herself in the presence of unexpected company. Fearful, she wanted to pretend it was merely her imagination and attempted to un-hear what was so apparent—but she heard it again.

She could sense her heart pound in her ears like the drums of her native land; vibrations rolled from the highest point of its curves as she approached the entry to the bedroom. Her fingertips throbbed; her toes burned as they bore the weight of her heavily cautious body. Something stirred again. She hid quickly behind the open door. The hall was clear, but the noise made it evident that someone else was with her. Her hands trembled anxiously for something to grab hold of, but nothing was there.

She silently glided into the hallway towards the kitchen,

and a woman whose physical stature could barely age her amongst teens, stood dressed in a lilac-colored apron near the stove. With one arm, she stirred a bubbling pot of grits; with the other, tucked away in a homemade sling, she attempted to reach for the salt that rested on the counter near her. She moaned softly when she overextended her reach, so pulled her arm back quickly to secure it.

Her name was Sophie, and before she could grab hold of the salt with her working arm, she noticed a shadow that loomed behind her. Startled, she nearly burned herself as she turned suddenly to face it head on. The two women gasped and shrieked.

"Oh my! I ain't mean tuh wake yah. I'm so sorry." Sophie pressed her palm against her chest as the newness of her sweet, southern dialect exploded in Laura's ears.

Incredibly distant, Laura asked, "What are you doing here? Who are you?"

"I'm sorry. They ain't tell yah?" She pulled up her apron to wipe her hands. "I'm Sophie. Sophie Carter."

Sophie moved closer to the frightened woman, extended her right hand, and for a moment interlocked it with Laura's. Sophie nervously nibbled at the inside of her mouth as she spoke.

"I usually keep up wit' tha place between visitors. Yah know, cleanin' and keepin' order. I told 'em I would assist wit' anything yah need, so I figured I'd start wit' breakfast."

Sophie was like an excited four-year-old who had prepared a tea party for mama and was anxious to be joined at the table. Laura watched her curiously.

Sophie pulled a chair for Laura. "Have a seat. I've been told I'm a good cook, but I don't know how it may be over in Africa, or what yah eat there fuh breakfast." A ceramic plate, encircled by a navy-blue line, was placed on the table in front of Laura. "I got some grits and eggs, and a couple pieces of bread." Sophie smiled.

Laura was puzzled, but she sat as Sophie explained. There was a thud, as if something had fallen in another room, and it interrupted Sophie. Both women looked in the direction of the hallway—where the sound had originated.

Laura stood. "What was that? Are you alone?"

Sophie nervously wiped her hand on the apron and stared in the direction of the noise. "No ma'am. I'm sorry. It's my baby. She's three. Umm—she usually comes along wit' me, but she won't be no trouble, I swear. She's a good girl."

"Then why do you have her locked in a room?"

"She barely locked in. Door's closed, is all. Knew she wouldn't sit so still out heah. Didn't wanna wake yah."

With caution, Laura said, "Well, I'm going to wash up, so I'll get her out here."

Laura walked down the narrow hallway and opened the first bedroom door. A young girl, whose height could only rival the length of a baseball bat, scurried across the room and hid in a corner. She tucked her head between her knees and sat quietly as Laura approached.

"Hey you." Laura stooped and reached out to touch the startled girl. The child raised her head just as Sophie burst into the room and moved swiftly towards her daughter, Rachel.

"Come on, gal. Always playin'." Sophie laughed nervously and ushered her daughter from the corner. "Let's not bother Ms. Laura. Come on out heah and eat some breakfast." Rachel took her mother's hand. Her hair had been twisted into several ponytails, and ribbons hang from each of them; they waved slightly with each of Rachel's motions.

After she splashed water onto her face and wiped it away with a hand towel, Laura took inventory of the morning's happenings as she stood before the mirror. When she rejoined the two at the kitchen table, Rachel had already begun to nibble away at the bread from her plate while Sophie waited politely.

"It looks good. Thank you," Laura said as she sat.

"I hope yah like it."

Laura took a bite of the buttered bread and chewed it completely before she asked, "Are you from here? Detroit?"

Sophie leaned in and reached for the fork that rested near her plate. "No, we came up—me and my husband—came up when Rachel wasn't born yet. We couldn't have her down in the south. Up heah is better." She settled into her chair, but not before she noticed the empty drinking glass near Laura's place setting. "I'm sorry. I didn't think tuh get yah somethin' tuh drink. Would yah like some water?"

"Please. No, I'm fine." Laura passed a spoonful of grits from her plate to her mouth. "Why all the apologies? I've only encountered two of you in this city, and you utter 'I'm sorry' with so much ease, and with so little reason to apologize." Laura stood from the table. "I can get my own water."

She walked into the kitchen, opened one cupboard door filled with plates, and then another filled with canisters of sugar, flour, and a few smaller vessels for spices. She finally landed on the cabinet that housed the drinking glasses and reached for one.

Sophie's searching expression dissolved as she released, "I don't know. I suppose we just wanna be right—tuh make other people feel right too."

Laura filled the glass with water from the faucet. "Seek to hear 'I'm sorry' less, and to say, 'thank you' more. That means you're being treated well." Laura glanced at the stove and took a sip of water. "And you managed to prepare all of this with one arm?"

Sophie chewed. "Yeah, it's nothin' really. We all have tuh eat."

Laura took her seat. "How did you injure your arm?"

Sophie's wiped her mouth with a napkin. "I'm sor—I mean, what did yah say?"

"I know I may be a challenge to understand. In time, I believe my words will resemble those you speak."

"Nah, yah not so hard tuh understand. Not as much as yah think anyway."

"I asked about your arm. How did it happen?"

Sophie chuckled. "I'm such a terrible sleepa'. I have night fits and all. Sometimes I just fall right on out. Ole clumsy me. This time it got my shoulder real good. I don't think it's broken, but being tied up like this takes the pressure off."

"Let me look at it. I can tell of your injuries."

"No need, Ms. Laura. I'll be just fine. Besides, yah travelled a great distance, and not tuh come and nurse on lil ole me. After breakfast, get yah rest. There's Friday night service, and Pastor Charles is expectin' yah tuh be ready. Now, if yah need anything, I'm here tuh help. I know these parts, and the people, so hopefully I can make it a lil' easier tuh get moving." The room quieted, and then Sophie spoke again, timidly. "Can I ask, what yah want us tuh call yah? I know you a princess and all, but people might look at us funny if I called yah that out loud," Sophie said with the warmest smile.

Laura looked pleasantly at Rachel, the tiny beauty who sat quietly and stuffed grits into her mouth. "Ms. Laura is fine. I don't have any titles here. I just come to do the work of the Lord."

"So, you a missionary? That's what we call people like that round heah."

"I am a woman on a mission—if that makes any sense." Sophie nodded, but had not fully grasped what Laura spoke of.

Three ebony girls sat in the quiet of the dining area and consumed the meal prepared by the Alabama woman. A slight breeze tussled the curtains, which drooped as eyelids over the windows on the far end of the room. The birds circled, and seemed to expect an invitation to enter; they stood perched on the window sill as the fragrance of a hearty meal was expelled from the apartment.

Time passed as they sat at the table and talked as most newly acquainted women. Laura listened attentively, and Sophie revealed that she had been married at seventeen. Her husband, Jeremiah, whom everyone called "Jack", had heard of opportunities for work in the north, and the two set out to raise their unborn child in conditions where fear would not become their guiding force in life.

"We didn't have much," Sophie said, "Our folks were born free, but had nothin' more tuh give us than life—and the white people threaten tuh take that too." Sophie explained, "But they allowed us tuh sell some of what we had, and then they held on tuh some things just tuh make sure we were good on our word. It would pay fuh the move here."

"And once you arrived?" Laura asked.

"Since we had tuh get our things back, and pay back the debt of 'em gettin' us heah, Jack found a job in a factory. Not many negroes there. But they say because he's strong as a bull, they could use 'em. He works hard, and don't give nobody no trouble either—well, unless they cross 'em—but of course he knows better than tuh ever go against a white man."

"What do you mean?" Laura picked up her drinking glass from the table and took a sip.

"He can be a little hard to reason wit' at times. He hears you, but he hears his own self more. Sometimes, that just gets in his way." Sophie looked away as though she had replayed an old memory. "Yeah, he's been that way fuh years."

Sophie noticed how engaged Laura had become, and she desired less of her attention. "Enough about me," Sophie said. "You must have many stories tuh tell."

"I have many years' worth," Laura responded. "And you will hear many of them in time. It seems that we should prepare for the evening." Laura looked towards the window where Rachel tapped gently to get a bird's attention, but it quickly flew away, and left the girl without a playmate. "The sun isn't so high."

"If I can help with anything, Ms. Laura, just call fuh me. I'll let yah know when the driver's outside."

"Thank you." Laura stood from the table and the blood in her legs began to properly circulate and adjust to her post-dormant form. "Are you coming with me?"

"Of course. I couldn't miss it."

Laura walked into the bedroom and closed the door behind herself. Before she removed a dress from her suitcase, she kneeled near the bed, and said a prayer.

# CHAPTER
# THREE

As she held Rachel's hand, Sophie became Laura's guide through the sanctuary. Over three hundred black faces were gathered tightly together—elbow to elbow—men, women, and little ones filled the church. Arms were raised in worship—extended as far as one could reach. Tears streamed from the eyes of weary mothers; the men watched for the leader to position himself.

The songstress at the front of the room bowed before the altar, and her voice amplified as Laura and Sophie approached her. Her words were given life through her toil and desperation, and it blossomed into the sweetest fruit that fed the souls of the worshippers.

"Gonna talk with the Prince of Peace," she sang.

And the others joined in, "Down by the riverside. Down by the riverside. Down by the riverside."

Laura noticed many who kneeled and found it difficult to speak. She could sense the heat of their breath as they released an alarming "hallelujah" and wept in agony—a sacrifice for the One who had seen them through.

"Gonna cross the river Jordan." The songstress arose and clapped to the tempo of the song—eyes closed in complete surrender, and in an atmosphere created by the worship of God's people.

"Down by the riverside. Down by the riverside. Down by the riverside."

And, as one body, they made a final declaration: "I ain't gonna study war no more. Study war no more. Ain't gonna study war no more."

Pastor Hezekiah Charles, dark and short in stature, took to the pulpit. Laura, Sophie, and Rachel located three wooden folding chairs at the front of the room that were set aside for them. An usher passed and raised an eyebrow as though to ensure the seats were occupied by its intended guests, and then slightly nodded to a man who stood near the pulpit.

"The Lord is a great deliverer," Pastor Charles bellowed. "He is a great way maker. He can tear down the walls, and build them up. Your praise can destroy every plot of wickedness. Praise God now, church. Praise Him!"

There was uproar as the people yelled God's praises. Soon, a well-dressed man, with an air of honor and prestige, approached Laura and spoke into her ear. She followed him up into the pulpit. Pastor Charles embraced her briefly and then extended his arm towards the podium—an invitation for her to speak. Laura was hesitant, yet knew she had an obligation to pour out a message for the thirsting believers gathered around her. She watched the crowd while she mustered the confidence to lean in to the microphone and speak.

"Your heart is pure, and your praise has power. More than that, your hands have power. Your minds have power. Your voice has power." The crowd clapped cautiously. "The power of God is within you. *You* are powerful." They clapped again—more assertively. "But what are you doing with your power?"

The crowd calmed quickly. Women found seats amongst the children; a few men stepped out into the aisles and stood along the walls of the sanctuary to hear her. Every hopeful eye watched curiously—to cling to every African syllable that rolled from Laura's tongue.

"I can hear God saying, 'What are you doing with your power? I am He who dwells within you. You are my people. You do not lack power, but you lack the understanding of what you have within you.' I am Laura Kofi, a representative from the Gold Coast. You have been a long time away from home. Africa. You are no longer prisoners of this place. Your brothers and sisters in Africa invite you home."

Most rode the Ferris wheel of Laura's words: from the height of her praise for God and the work the men and women had successfully done, and then descended to their need to do more. They moved fluidly between conviction and inspiration, but the thought of a return to Africa left many of them baffled. And Laura noticed.

"Africa. It is a land you have never known, but it is home. It has many places that are not unlike this country, with your conveniences and your tools. It is beautiful beyond imagination, and God would have it be as perfect as He made it—even this day. And He is calling for His people to operate in the power of His might, and to come to know your home."

She continued, "But for now we're here in this place. Power doesn't cower in the corner, or settle for desolation and scraps, or is consistently cautious and fearful instead of moving joyfully in love. The God within you is great. And greater than those who cause you to be afraid. Greater is He that is within *you*. He *is* within you. His power is operating through you. What have you done with your power?"

Laura spoke for another fifteen minutes, pulled scriptures from the Bible to support her claims of God's desire to see His people prosper peacefully. After every word had been spent, she turned from the podium and was joined by Pastor Charles who gently shook her hand and escorted her down the platform. The energy moved from spark to flame, and Pastor Charles was not ready to quench it, so he approached the pulpit to reinforce Laura's message.

"So, what are you doing with your power?" he fanned the embers of their praise. "The power of God is unlike any other." He continued to speak as Laura stepped down. A breeze from an open window swept across the sweat of her neck and a chill ensued. Before she reached her seat, she was approached by a woman. Sophie, who stood close by, watched as the woman drew nearer.

The woman asked, "Can we talk?" Laura looked to Sophie and nodded in approval of the woman's request. "I could really use your help."

Sophie escorted them to a quieter room—what seemed to be a meeting chamber, or nursery, or lounging space, whatever it was best used for in any given moment. The sounds of service continued to reverberate in the space, but the women disconnected from the fellowship and focused on the stranger's cause.

"I've come here from Chicago. Our city's leaders aren't doing much of anything to help us there," she said dreadfully.

Laura asked, "What's taking place?"

The woman spoke slowly, "In my city a few years ago, a boy from the neighborhood was swimming in an area for whites. They threw rocks at him, and he drowned."

"I heard about that—all over the papers," Sophie interrupted as she gently tugged at one of Rachel's ponytails.

The woman continued without acknowledging Sophie's interjection. "Afterwards, there were riots for weeks on end. Whites against blacks, police, women. They burned many of our homes. It's been nearly five years now, and many people still don't have homes or work. I heard what you said about power. My people need to hear you. They need a little push to do what needs doing. They've given up."

Nothing more was required to be spoken. Laura heard

the call, and she desired to answer it.

~

By morning, Laura was on a train to another unfamiliar city. She toured the areas of Chicago most impacted by the riots—those that faced incredible economic hardship. As they rode along, a guide articulated the struggle of the community.

"His name was Eugene Williams. They killed him, and no one was charged. The cost of a black man swimming over an invisible line." The guide looked from the window and tapped it slightly with her fingernail.

Laura noticed the decayed town. "All the buildings, the homes, they're just burnt frames. Why are they not rebuilt by now?"

"After the riots, the white man was afraid. They banned all the Negroes from returning to the stockyard. More than fifteen thousand people were without work, and many of them never found another opportunity much better than that one."

"You can lose any material thing and still press through; but God forbid you lose hope," Laura whispered. The car pulled up to a small community center surrounded by a dust lot on Chicago's south side.

The people had already gathered—stuffed, and as intricately layered as laid bricks, one wedged closely to another. It was standing room only, yet people continued to trickle in. A dense stench saturated the space and pointed a finger at the dwelling's poor ventilation and the lack of basic commodities of its inhabitants. Laura mounted a small platform and prepared to address the crowd, and the room went silent; those present were aware of the absence of anything to amplify her words, and knew that heavy breaths, a sneeze or cough, or a mere *hush* to calm a restless infant would mean the loss of a moment, a word, or a lesson they so eagerly desired to learn.

Among those who awaited Laura's conversational perspective was a fair-skinned, black man of grand stature. He towered over those who stood near him. His name was Allan. He and Maxwell, a man with a dark, hostile countenance, were both representatives of the group organized by Marcus Garvey—the Universal Negro Improvement Association—the UNIA for short. The two men were pressed against a wall in the tight space and casually listened.

The heat continued to rise as people piled in. To limit their torment, Laura opened her mouth and spoke with compassion.

"Accept my words with love; my heart is to see you live out each of your days in the way God intended. What I see here are people living in a way that perpetuates the weakness by which you've been labeled. The white oppressor is wrong in judgement, and morals. You are not what they say you are." She gulped the saliva accumulated in her mouth to make room for what she would say next. "And you—you complain that there aren't enough jobs. You complain that there isn't sufficient housing. You complain about the law and its enforcers. You complain about unfairness, the targets you consistently wear on your backs as you struggle to merely survive. How could you complain about that which you comply and conform? You are living beneath your means. Your hands must do the work. Your voice must be the change. Your power must be made known. Don't cower in the crevices of a community left in shambles. It is time to re-build, and to build beyond what's already here. It is time to prosper. Allow your pain to push you. Allow God's power to sustain you."

At the mention of the Spirit-Being, Maxwell, arms folded and pressed tightly to his torso, looked to Allan with disgust. The Jamaican-born leader, and captain of the African Black Legion—the UNIA's uniformed branch, spoke to his partner. "The UNIA can't use a preacher. We need business-minded, intellectual leaders," Maxwell said. Allan nodded in agreement.

A man in the crowd stood at Laura's pause and respectfully removed his hat, which revealed his balding head. "What do we do?" he asked with a raspy voice. "They won't hire many of us around here. And we don't have the money to just up and leave." He clenched his hat tightly.

"You don't have the money?" Laura responded.

"No ma'am."

"And you don't have work?"

"No ma'am," he said. "The whites have it all."

"And what do you have?" The man visibly thought of a proper response. Laura added, "And that which you have, you give away. When you need soap, where do you buy? When you need food, where do you buy? When you learn to buy and sell right here within your own community, you will employ, you will build, you will have."

What Laura spoke was understood, and heads nodded, which created a visible wave of agreement that swept across the crowd; a few listeners gave her response a subtle applause. Allan stood fully erect from the wall, intrigued. His response did not go unnoticed. With a grim expression, Maxwell locked eyes on his partner as Laura's words lured Allan from his relaxed posture.

"And how do you suppose we get there?" the man asked.

"Begin to make your own. Learn to make your own clothing, toiletries, to grow your own gardens. We buy only from each other. We grow, expand, and hire each other—right here. And then, let us not forget our brothers and sisters in Africa who are eager to trade with you here in America, to build here *and* there. And return. Return to Mother Africa."

Skeptical, the man returned a loud "tis" coupled with a smirk as his head shook in objection.

"Now, see, I've heard enough people talk about Africa. We never been there. We don't have the pennies to get to the county line, but somehow getting over to Africa is possible." He paused. "Tell me how to survive right here in Chicago. This is all I know." He turned to gain the approval of the crowd. Many looked to Laura for her response, and some agreed with his stance and offered an unyielding "um hm".

"If survival is all you want," she said, "you don't require much. I can give you fish to eat today, or I can teach you to get your own and you'll never hunger. I can teach you with a rod, but you can feed others if you invest in a boat and a net. You choose, but whatever you choose, commit wholeheartedly."

Several people whispered amongst the crowd, and many were completely captured by Laura's inspiring message. Allan applauded her presentation, but Maxwell held his initial position and refused to budge from the wall that had propped him up since the start of the meeting.

It was near sunset when the third speaker of the afternoon offered his perspective on the state of the community. Laura had been the only woman invited to speak, and the one the crowd found most engaging as observed by their consistent claps and an occasional "that's right". And if that was not enough of an indication, the women who desired to greet her following the event, waited patiently for up to fifteen minutes at a time to avoid intrusion while Laura interacted with others.

One woman requested prayer for her toddler who had suffered through several seizures. The young mother could not afford proper medical care, and was desperate. Laura took the boy into her arms and cradled him tightly as she prayed, and then released him back to his mother.

The spirit of God ran through her like a consistent current of electricity from a power source. She was not only ready to do whatever He instructed, and to go where ever He would guide, she was eager, nearly anxious, to follow as He commanded. Laura's journey to America had not been an easy feat; she engaged in a spiritual tug-o-war as she resisted the call. Once there, she sensed the needs of the people, and knew they thirsted for a word from God. She was then made alive, vibrant, a spark ready to burst into flame at God's call.

Several attendees who lived in homes near the community center went to the kitchen for a hearty meal— some cornbread and greens and whatever had been left of a meatloaf from the day before—all food donated by a local church to those who could not regularly provide food for their families. When it was all gone, and the elderly cook noticed Laura had not eaten, she pulled a cabbage and some carrots from a wooden crate and chopped them.

Laura sat at a table and slowly thumbed through her bible. She ate from a small plate of fruit as she waited for the cook to scrounge up what she could for a proper meal.

As Laura absorbed a psalm into every penetrable space of her thoughts, she was interrupted by the voices of men who passed near the room. One of the voices lingered as the others quickly became distant and faint. The strong, commanding voice could claim anyone's attention, but Laura did not stir. She attempted to obliterate the distraction with more focus, and believed it would soon be gone.

"Alright fellas," the voice spoke. "Have a good night. I'll be down in Florida soon enough." The bang of a closed door vibrated through the room.

Allan walked into the kitchen and gently rubbed the cook's shoulders before he snatched a slice of carrot from the chopping board and popped it into his mouth. As he chewed, he noticed her—Laura—as she sat quieter than he had first encountered her.

He kissed the elderly cook on her cheek, grabbed another slice of carrot, and began to crunch—a lure for Laura's attention. He failed. He poured himself a glass of water from the pitcher on the counter, and walked over to where Laura chewed quietly on a wedge of succulent melon.

Allan spoke gently, "I don't mean to impose…"

"Thank you," she responded, and reached for another slice of fruit.

He paused to acknowledge the apparent dismissal, but he continued. "It's just that what you speak of aligns completely with the goals of the UNIA, and I would like…"

Laura looked at him. "I thought your goal was to *not* impose," she said in a voice too sweet to count it rude. "This room is quietest. And I chose it for study. If I must find another, please let me know."

"No, stay here. I'll leave."

"I do not mean to offend you. I just must be filled before I can pour."

Allan was puzzled.

Laura continued, "Like that glass you hold. Its purpose is to get the water from its source to your lips for your benefit. It has no purpose empty. While God can fill us one by one and we can drink directly from a well or spigot, there are some glasses, vessels, that God pours into. We pour out to meet the need, and people no longer thirst. But one day, they learn to drink directly from the pitcher. You know what happens then?

Allan leaned in a little closer, captivated. "What?"

"Germs and contamination," she whispered as though she had offered something profound, and then giggled a little to herself. Allan backed away with a grin that could have its own area code, and contributed to the laughter. "I'm joking. Well, at least about that part."

Allan extended his hand to shake hers. "I'm Allan Gregory. I work primarily out of Miami, Florida, live in Jacksonville, but I've been up here for a few weeks now."

"I am not familiar. What distance is Florida?" she asked, and her accent was a reminder of her reasonable unfamiliarity.

"A great way from here," Allan said as he placed the drinking glass on the table. "You'll have to pass through a lot of ugly to get to the beauty of the south." He paused and cleared his throat. "The Universal Negro Improvement Association is strong, and getting stronger. Just like you spoke of, our mission is to build our own communities and excel in commerce and trade. We've built more enterprises, opened business, trained entire communities, and employed nearly a thousand of our own with our organization."

"I've heard briefly of your program. And it sounded very much like the advertisement I hear now."

"UNIA is strong, with millions on board to carry out its vision."

"And with a leader facing years in prison." She locked eyes with Allan who quickly picked through words like rotting berries to explain.

"Merely evidence of the white man's fear. They will remove anyone they fear—simple as wiping smut from a surface. If it's potent enough though, it will always leave residue."

"Where would someone like me be of use?"

"All over," he answered boldly. "In this country, your voice should be heard everywhere, but there is no place like the south. Even if you haven't seen much of it yet, the UNIA has a strong presence in the north; but in the south, the people have managed to hold themselves in captivity despite being freed." His tone became melancholy. "Treat people like they're not human long enough, some people start to believe it."

"There is no battleground like the mind's."

"I would say the south is quite comparable."

Laura removed a slip of paper from the back of her bible. She read the print as she reached for a writing utensil. "I must return to Detroit soon. And here is a list of places and people that are expecting me." She wrote the information down. "I will leave you with my address. Before leaving for Florida, please notify me. I will lift it in prayer."

Laura handed him the paper and stood to leave the room. She shook his hand. "It was a pleasure," she said, and walked away. She left her bible open on the table. Allan casually turned a page or two as he watched her walk out of the room. He guessed she would return, and would expect for him to no longer be there. He accepted the passing thought as truth, and compliantly walked away.

# CHAPTER
# FOUR

After a delayed, early morning train, Laura was anxious for rest. By the time she reached Michigan Central Station, her feet throbbed and pulsated, yet they pushed forward in great anticipation to no longer carry the weight. The driver who awaited her train's arrival let her off at the front door, and she let herself into the apartment.

Two pots rested on the stove—still warm with morning oatmeal and raisins. Laura sniffed the sweet air, and then dropped her bag at the hall's opening. More enticing than brown sugar and butter on a bowl of hot oats was the melodic voice that enveloped Laura and, in her mind's eye, postured her for immediate worship.

"It is well with my soul. It is well. It is well with my soul" filled the atmosphere—took full control, and commanded every speck of dust to sway in still air.

Laura passed an open bedroom door where Rachel napped on the bed. She continued to the bathroom, and lingered near the origin of the voice. The sound was painted with sadness and travail. Laura's nose tingled as emotion welled up within her. While entertained, she found it difficult to be uplifted, and was burdened instead—suffocating on the dense smog that escaped the bathroom and occupied the hallway.

Sophie sang, "Whatever my lot, thou hast taught me to know it is well, it is well, with my soul." Laura was the unexpected audience, and immediate supporter, of the woman behind the voice, but a prisoner of its substance. She continued to listen.

The knob rattled and the door opened abruptly. Sophie emerged and was startled by Laura's presence. She grabbed the loose towel and pulled herself back into the bathroom, and out of Laura's sight.

"Oh my! Ms. Laura!" she panted. "Yah have tuh stop scarin' me. I can't do this. I thought yah would still be in Chicago." She reemerged. Sophie tightened the towel that adorned her delicate body.

Laura smiled at Sophie's reaction, and concealed that her song had been a source of entertainment in the moments leading to their encounter. Laura inspected the woman who clung tightly to her towel. Sophie's chest continued to rise and fall in the aftershock of fear as she attempted to catch a smooth, leveling breath.

Laura's smile quickly faded. The markings of Sophie's body were of a hue as deep as plum—and just as large as one in some places. Other markings had begun to fade, and were gray, as blood vessels fought to flourish in its proper place and against the damage that had been done. From her shoulder, to her neck and arms, Laura gave Sophie's body a brief once-over. Sophie finally noticed the great measure of her exposure, and she quickly adjusted her towel. She lifted it towards her neck and wrapped herself as though it were a cape.

Sophie spoke nervously, eyes lowered, head tilted slightly, "I gotta do better wit' this sleepin' thing, Ms. Laura.

I'm startin' tuh think I'm best off just sleepin' on the flo'."
She smiled with great discomfort.

Laura's tone was serious, "You might be better off
down there. That is, unless you have fleas." Sophie was
bewildered. Laura continued, "It appears you have a dog."

Sophie slid past Laura and tottered towards the
bedroom. "No, Ms. Laura. What make yah think that? I
don't. I'm gonna figure it out and I'll get better." Sophie
walked into the room and closed the door behind herself.

With forced acceptance, Laura moved away from the
scene of confrontation, and sought rest in her bedroom.

Hours later, as the wind brushed along the windows,
which made subtle popping sounds as the hinges rebelled
against its force, and crickets chirped in celebration of
darkness, Laura's sleep was interrupted by the sound of
Sophie's wails. Periodically muffled, Laura sensed that
Sophie intended to contain herself, but failed significantly.
As she laid there, with aches of her travels, she became
burdened with the travail of her new neighbor—a woman
whose spirit was sweeter than the ripest fruit, but whose
sorrow left a rotten stain on those who cared for her.

In darkness, Laura prayed, "God, give her the strength
that only You can. Give her the boldness that will cause
every enemy to flee."

The streak of moonlight revisited the path through
Laura's bedroom, and she was comforted as Sophie's wails
ceased.

~

Fatigue subsided, Laura washed the sleep from her
eyes in the bathroom. Sophie and a strange woman, whose
hair swept neatly from her face in large ringlets, stood near
the end of the hallway. The woman carried a duffle bag, and
shifted it from her right hand into her left as if to free a hand
to greet Laura.

"Good mornin', Ms. Laura!" Sophie exclaimed. "This

here is Kenya. She was sent tuh do yah hair this mornin'—get yah ready for revival meetin'. We just thought wit' yah being in front of so many people, yah might wanna look yah best. Besides, yah went to bed so early, I figured you'd be tired, and could use somebody tuh do yah hair. And since I ain't no good at it—ta dah!" She motioned towards Kenya who politely allowed the introduction.

Laura caressed the strands of her "morning do" and was comforted by Sophie's suggestion. "Yes, please." She moved towards a chair already positioned at the kitchen table.

"Yah hungry?" Sophie asked. "I can make yah somethin' hot to eat."

"I'm just fine. Still a little tired. Appetite not as strong as usual." Laura looked around the room. "Where is Rachel?"

A tumultuous ocean of emotion instantly overtook Sophie who stopped in her tracks and exhaled deeply as if to posture herself properly before she responded. "Her father come fuh her last night. Yah know, he just wanna look after her while I'm working heah."

Laura sensed a lie.

Sophie walked into the kitchen and manipulated a few pots. With the clangor came the reminder of her fleeting peace.

"When will she return?" Laura called out.

"Hopefully, by evenin'. I'm makin' her favorite fuh dinner." Sophie placed an apron around her waist. "Some fried chicken and green beans." As she tied it tightly, she suddenly found it unbearable to stand. "'Scuse me." Sophie left the kitchen, rushed into the bedroom and closed the door. There was silence.

Laura rested on the faith of answered prayer, and sat high in the chair for Kenya's hands to go to work. Kenya separated the loose sections of Laura's dark, coiled hair with a comb.

"I've heard so much about you. Sophie has really taken

a liking to you, and all the work you do." She combed as gently as she possibly could. "My mama named me Kenya after the country in Africa. She said she would never be able to go, but she assumed it was a beautiful place." Kenya was an unapologetic fast-talker.

"And she is right. 'Beautiful savannas that stretch beyond the eye, mountains that kiss the sky,'" Laura recited. "I've never been to the region, but we hear stories as children. Poetry and folktales."

Kenya ran her fingers through Laura's mane. "I'm hoping for the day I'll get to see it. But for now, let's see to it that this hair is nice for the event." She turned away and lifted her duffle bag from the floor. She removed a hot comb and walked over to the stove—still warm from the fire Sophie had lit for breakfast preparations. Laura watched curiously as Kenya placed the comb on the stove, which became increasingly hot after she shifted the wood that burned beneath it. After a minute or so, she returned with a smoking comb.

Laura shifted her head away from the woman. "What is that for?"

"I'm going to make your hair nice and straight." The ribbons of smoke continued to rise from the comb in her hand. "You'll be just like one of the women from the magazines," Kenya said assuredly.

With startling authority, Laura said, "Put it down."

Without question, Kenya carried the comb back into the kitchen, and placed it on the cool counter.

Laura asked, "What's wrong with my hair?"

At that moment, Sophie resurfaced fresh-faced and reenergized to see the cause of the commotion—eyes still a gentle shade of pink.

Laura continued, "Is it not beautiful as God made it?"

Sophie chimed in, "We just wanna give yah some options, Ms. Laura. Just somethin' different, a change."

Laura gently lowered her head and allowed an audible breath to escape her parted lips. She leaned in, pressed her elbows against the table, and clasped her hands together in a final motion. She pondered aloud, "In what *other* ways have you striven to have options?"

The two women looked to each other and trusted the other would speak.

Laura continued, "You settle here in this community, but you seek options here." Laura pointed to her hair and the women's eyes followed. "We can change our hair but not the condition of our homes. We see beauty in things we don't have, seek it, and mimic it with as much success as each breath, but we see dilapidated neighborhoods, lack of a thriving economy on this side of the city, poor schools where kids can't even learn for lack of sufficient heating, but we don't seek to match and exceed the thriving white communities, their adequate school buildings, their levels of ownership. You set your mind on beauty and adornments to feel good about living in such ugliness."

Laura lowered her arms in wait of what the women would say. They were silent.

Kenya broke the silence and approached Laura again. "I can just do something really nice, and without the straightening comb."

Laura's words were foreign. The women were conditioned to merely create beauty where they could, and never stretched themselves to believe beauty should be created even where they thought they could not. Their actions aligned with their thoughts and beliefs, and were limited. They could not accept Laura's reprimand straightaway; the discomfort of the truth required them to search themselves after they peeled back resentment brought upon them by immediate offense. But they were open.

With a few hours to spare before the evening's events, and Laura's ploy to remove Sophie from the window in wait of Rachel's return, she suggested they head out for a while.

With minimal pedestrian traffic on a Wednesday evening, they walked a mile together and took a seat in the colored section of a streetcar. They approached a heavily populated community of black men and women who stood outside a string of storefronts with a restaurant on its tail end, and a small theatre plopped in the center. Laura's eyes widened.

"Should we get off here?" she asked, but stood before the other women could answer. They followed suit.

The streetcar passed as the women waited to cross the road. The environment into which they had been submerged was the speck of light that brought Laura alive.

"There are so many black people here," Laura said.

"This here is UNIA, Ms. Laura. Businesses owned by its members. Only employs its own," Sophie said.

"Is that so?"

"Yes ma'am." She pointed, "That there is a drug store owned by Mr. and Mrs. Ralph Edwards. Been open about two years. The theater been open just as long. They use it fuh meetin's most times, but they even have classes and plays fuh the children. Always open." Sophie fully realized the success of her community as she continued to explain its various components. "That restaurant there has the best sandwiches around. And there is a fuel station tucked off a lil' on that end."

"I now wonder why blacks continue to buy from the whites across the tracks—in a place they're not wanted."

Kenya chimed in, "Well, Ms. Laura, the nickel each of us spent to get on the streetcar to get over here could be all someone has to buy what they need."

"If we build more, more people will have access."

"That could be true, but we have to keep in mind that the whites don't like too much black progress. They'll tolerate a nugget of blacks doing okay for themselves, but they've shut down some other shops as quickly as they were opened."

"It's one thing to teach the people to unify and to prosper, and it's another to teach them to protect themselves," Laura reasoned. "That's why Africa is where

35

we should all seek to live—in total freedom, with unlimited opportunity to be as great as the God who created us. And fearless."

"Africa seems so far from here," Kenya spoke. "And protect? Black people can't defend themselves—not if they want peace. I heard that in the south the KKK and the UNIA have some sort of agreement. They want everything separate—let blacks build for blacks, and let whites alone. Not sure how true it is, but it would make sense." She shrugged.

The women enjoyed hot beef sandwiches at the counter of the restaurant and watched children run freely from the drugstore after they purchased a few lollipops and chocolates to appease their sugar-tites, and then they set off for home to prepare for service.

Laura had finally experienced firsthand the success of Garvey's organization, and she yearned to see more, experience more, build more. On the ride home, her eyes darted the undeveloped land—high grass and untamed brush—as she imagined new communities of black homes, black schools that would teach black children, black shops that would replenish the goods in the black homes that would later employ the black children who would graduate from the black schools. Her mind seemed to wander, but she did not lack focus.

~

The months passed quickly, just as a train would rush by a man who stood in wait. An entire season came and went, and Laura's reach had extended to six states surrounding Detroit. Laura was either speaking, or on her way to speak, and she was graced with the strength to endure the needs of the people she would influence.

The voice of God spoken through her inspired the people to build new storehouses, to demand better quality conditions for schools, or if their requests fell on deaf ears, rally together and pool their resources to do what was necessary. Her undying spark lit a flame in every community that dared to invite her—and they became productive, peaceful, passionate people.

The glory of God that rested on Laura seemed to amplify as the size of the crowd that turned out to see her made a steady climb from a few hundred to over a thousand in a single setting. Laura would raise her bible into the air, and shake it as if to emphasize its power, and people would offer up a praise that caused their legs to buckle beneath them.

Not everyone was pleased with Laura's message, and not because it was harmful or unnecessary for the time. Her voice and her message were so magnetic that she would empty several sanctuaries in cities where she would appear to share a word. Clergy in various cities would show up to their perspective places of worship and were greeted by empty pews. Meanwhile, Laura's greatest task was to ensure the people would have enough chairs to sit if their legs grew weary—but no one who stood, even for hours at a time, ever once complained.

When Laura arrived home after a few days away, she found a sealed envelope addressed to her on the floor near the front door. She opened it immediately, and it read: *I am leaving for Florida in a week. We could use you in the south. I hope you can join me. Allan.*

She stared off into the distance, folded the letter, and walked into the room where she had prayed what seemed ten thousand prayers the previous months, and then closed the door.

# CHAPTER
## FIVE

With the growing sunlight, Laura found herself immersed in reflection as she stood on a riverbank not even a mile's walk from the apartment—a place she frequented when time would permit. She sought peace for the journey, but was met with tinges of discomfort and anxiety, which she assumed was the stirring fear of the unknown.

She delicately placed her hand on top of the water, sensed its pulse, and the two quietly connected. Laura breathed deeply, emptied every inch of toxic thought, and felt the water cleanse more than her hand—but each impurity that lingered longer than she would naturally allow. After a few minutes, she lifted her hand from the water, and whispered, "Amen."

Once home, Sophie assisted Laura and packed toiletries neatly inside a cream-colored suitcase with mahogany stripes that bordered on either end. The bedroom was silent, aside from the occasional shuffle of clothing or glass bottles that clattered together. Both women contemplated what would be next for them. After months in each other's company, neither desired to part with the other.

"I'm gone miss yah, Ms. Laura," Sophie placed a scarf into the suitcase and interrupted the silence. "Just one more day. How long yah goin' fuh?"

"I don't know. However the Lord leads."

Sophie sat gently on the bed. "That's what I love most about yah. Yah just so, so free—can go and do however God calls."

Laura folded a skirt and placed it into her bag. "We can all do that."

"Well, not me, Ms. Laura," Sophie responded. "Us married women have to answer to our men. When he say we can't go, we can't."

Laura sat next to Sophie. "But your husband is quite alright with you being here most nights?" Sophie nodded her head. "Doesn't seem like you're together much."

"I know. Sometimes he just needs some space, and I'd rather give it to 'em than to—than to…" Sophie's eyes lowered, weighted by the shame of her near-confession.

"*That* is fear," Laura said pointedly.

Sophie chuckled to herself. "I can't just up and leave 'em. I'm married. I got my baby tuh think about."

"Staying makes it evident that you're *not* thinking of your baby. Don't make her the scapegoat of your fear. You are responsible for her—even when you choose not to live responsibly for you."

"But there ain't nothin' in the Word that says I can leave 'em. I would be wrong." Sophie stood and walked towards the dresser to collect more of Laura's things. "And downright outta order," she spoke with her back turned to Laura.

Laura continued to pack blouses into the suitcase as she spoke. "The tool intended to set people free has also been a tool to keep people in bondage." Sophie turned to face

Laura. "God loves you, and He loves your baby. He wants you to live. The Word doesn't take the place of good, common sense."

Sophie lowered her head, and then looked towards the window. "But where would I go?" As she considered her innocent child, she grasped the tip of her thumb and slightly tugged on it. "How will I take care of Rachel?"

"And *there* is where you trust God. That is where you're free. Pray."

Laura stuffed additional items into her bag as Sophie sat in total contemplation until she finally rendered herself useless and asked to be excused. Solemn, Sophie walked out of the bedroom, and the front door of the apartment was heard as it shut behind her.

Laura could not know how God would work out Sophie's situation, but she trusted He would, and that the change would be favorable. She prepared herself to be without the woman who had been at her side those previous months as she travelled, planned to travel, or would rest from her travels, but she was grateful for the season to serve alongside her.

Anticipation for the journey to the south was overshadowed by the cloud of goodbyes between Laura and Sophie, so Laura prayed, "Father in heaven, equip me for the journey. Align each step. Send to me those who will purpose to do Your will in the earth."

After the clasp of the suitcases were finally forced into a locked position, Laura placed them near the entryway and sat near the window in the living room—quiet goodbyes. She watched men and women come and go along the road that ran parallel to her apartment. They moved with the energy of one on a mission, but once they encountered another person or two, they stopped and spoke, and returned to their initial position and never progressed beyond the road, or the stoop, or their own minds, stagnant and hopeless.

It was almost noon when a car pulled up outside, and

the knots in Laura's belly tightened. Nausea ensued with each step towards the door. Dizziness followed. Heat radiated from her exposed arms, a tingle provoked her hands to sweat. She finally stood close enough to grab her bags, but she took one final glance back into the unoccupied room before her clammy palms lifted them from the floor.

Allan met Laura on the front stoop once she made sure the apartment had been adequately secured; she did not know when Sophie would return. The sun revealed the depth of Allan's green eyes, which glistened as he greeted Laura and reached out to take her bags. The two descended the steps together in silence—both unaware of what the future would hold, but both had committed to leave a firm mark on America's foundation, and on the future of the black race.

Allan broke the silence as he opened the car door. "I'm happy you've chosen to join us. We'll have a few stops along the way, but we should reach Miami in a few days."

"I trust that I am in good hands," Laura responded.

"I can guarantee that you are. I'm a great driver. Real safe too."

"I was talking about God." Laura smirked. Allan shifted to close the door when a striking voice was heard in the distance.

"Ms. Laura!" Sophie was spotted; she carried Rachel on her hip as she clung tightly to a bag. "Wait! Ms. Laura!"

She panted, and sweat cascaded down each of her thick sideburns and onto the collar of her blouse. She placed her daughter's feet on the ground next to the vehicle and rested her hand against the hood of the car.

Mystified, Laura examined Sophie's condition and desired to help. "Breathe, child," she said.

Allan stared at the woman who struggled to synchronize her breath.

Sophie said, "Sir, I know yah don't know me, but if I could come along," she paused and took in another breath. "I promise I could help—wit' almost anything." She let out one long *hufffff*, and picked up the bag that had fallen near her feet.

Laura's eyes lit up and she smiled faintly. When Allan noticed, he said, "Well, if Ms. Laura is alright with it—." Laura nodded to indicate her approval. "Then I suppose we can have you two along."

Relieved, yet still in a battle to gain her composure, Sophie grabbed her daughter by the hand, kissed her cheek and smiled brightly. Allan opened the door for both ladies to climb inside.

"This gone be good. I just know it," Sophie said excitedly as she settled into her seat.

~

The group coasted over terrain that varied from rocky to smooth, and back to rocky again. The brightness of the stars in the night sky kept Laura's attention, but a quick nudge caused her to break her focus and place it on the driver— who she detected had grown exhausted. Allan nodded off a little, but quickly grabbed at the wheel when he noticed his apparent fatigue.

Laura gently touched his hand, an indication that she had seen what he attempted to hide. "Should we pull over?" she offered.

"I'm just fine. A little tired, but we have some ways to go. We'll be stopping in Tennessee. There are some kind folks there. They own a little farm, and they have enough room for all of us. I expect to be there in another hour or so."

"I can understand how exhausted you must be—having such little rest."

"Yeah," he thought a second, "but it's nothing to keep me awake. A little conversation would do."

Laura wanted to assist in whatever way she could, so contemplated a moment. "Where are you from?"

"I was born in Connecticut. That's north."

"Do you still have family there?" she inquired.

"Grandma." He smiled at the thought of her. "She's an old woman, but still the most beautiful soul a man could know. Born a slave, but even after freedom, she didn't move too far from where she'd spent those days. I have an aunt and some cousins up there too; they look after her."

"What about your mother?"

He scratched his forehead with his pinky finger. "My mama was never a slave." He exhaled deeply. "She actually belonged to a family who owned them. She was white. And my daddy, a Negro born to a slave mother."

There was a bump in the road, and the two bounced a little in their seats. Laura steadied herself with a grip of the car door. "You alright?" Allan asked.

"Just fine." She released her grasp and sat at ease. "Keep going. I'm listening."

Hesitantly, he began again, "My grandma was mammy to the Massa's children. So, she raised them right along with my daddy up until she was free. Even after she was no longer their property, she kept working—just for a place to sleep and to care for her children. Her husband, my grandfather, had died not long after my aunt was born. No other signs than his heart stopped in the night. Left Grandma alone to fend for herself."

"Perhaps he had grown weary—exhausted."

"Grandma told me he hadn't been the same leading up to the day he died. Something just off about him. Didn't complain of any pain. No sickness either. She said he was as loving as they'd always known him to be."

"It's always good to be left with good memories of those we love. How did your grandmother get along after he was gone?"

"Like she always had—with hard work. She was always taking care of Missus' children, and helped with the upkeep of the big house. When ole Massa died of fever, he left his wife the house—but she didn't know much about maintaining it, so my grandmother became essential to taking care of the property and all the people in it."

"Even your mother."

"Yes. My mother wasn't but eighteen when, just a year or so after her father died, her mother died too. And the story goes, there was some time between when Missus died, and when my mother was sent to live with her aunt and uncle in New York, where she and my daddy got real close. Grandma told me a story about how my daddy was out trimming the hedges near the big house, and my mother would see to it that he had cold water to drink."

"What's so wrong with that?" Laura inquired.

"It wasn't her duty. Whites didn't concern themselves with the needs of niggers—not now, and not back then— no matter how much they'd taken a liking to them. Grandma knew then that sweet eyes had fallen on Daddy, but it was no stopping them. Grandma said she tried to get him to keep good distance, but my hard-headed daddy just let it be."

"So, what happened?"

"I'm here," Allan chuckled. "My mother went to live off on her own in a town near Grandma after the big house was sold. When she went into labor, she sent for her. They say she must've delivered me by herself and wouldn't let anyone near, but I don't believe that. Grandma said by the time she'd made it to her, it had been at least two days since I was born, and no one had been to see about her. She wasn't in good shape. But Grandma fixed her up, like she'd always done, and got her better in time."

"Where's your mother now?"

"She handed me over to Grandma not long after I was born, and she disappeared. Some say she moved back to New York. It don't matter much. I don't know a white woman who would claim to have a nigger for a son."

"And your father?"

"Kept his distance. Grandma said he became fearful after learning what he'd done, getting a white girl pregnant. I would see him when he visited, but I had to call him Uncle

Richard. He never wanted anyone to know, and even after all these years."

Laura's forehead tightened with compassion. "It must have been difficult for you as a boy."

"I fought a lot. White boys couldn't come near me, and black boys didn't like my complexion, the way my hair curled loosely, or these eyes—they couldn't stand to imagine how they'd measure up to me with this bright skin, and with the learning Grandma drilled into me day in and day out. I could read and write early on, and was smart too. I guess their thinking was that I had more than enough white attention to need theirs. They were wrong. They would call me names. So, fight is what I'd do. I fought myself right into jail a few times. Met a man named James Nimmo after I was released a few years ago who sold me on the UNIA, and it changed my life. Gave me something meaningful to fight for."

Allan shared several accounts of his UNIA involvement, trials, and accomplishments. Laura listened and took note of what she would soon encounter herself. She was hopeful, and believed God had orchestrated the moment. She remained peaceful and optimistic.

Time passed quickly. Allan glanced into the back seat where Sophie and Rachel slept. "Enough of my tales. What about you?"

Matter-of-factly Laura said, "I am a woman of faith, and I am in this country to follow God's lead."

Allan sat quietly. He assumed she would say more, but nothing came. "I guess that's simple enough."

"You want more? There isn't much."

"You ever married?"

"No," she said sweetly. "It was always my heart to help people. I didn't see the need. My father gave me the freedom to choose. The poor marry young. I had the option."

Allan steered the car onto a road lined with gravel. Although dark, the lantern on the log-cabin illuminated the front porch, and the car soon came to a stop.

"We made it, Ms. Laura."

A dark figure stood in the doorway in anticipation for the guests. And as each of them exited the vehicle, they stretched slightly and straightened their garments to become more presentable for their hosts.

~

After a night of rest, the crew did not delay a moment to continue towards Florida. By the time the sun was high enough to light the roadway, they were already on the second leg of their journey.

About an hour in, Allan grew curious about the woman and child who joined them on the trip south. He knew little about Sophie; she had slept most of the previous day's trip and did not speak much. Each time she addressed him in any way, she would turn her head away from him, or place her hands somewhere near her face as if to shield it. It was when she dozed off in the sunlight as she rode in the backseat that he finally learned what she had concealed.

"Is the girl in some kinda' trouble?" Allan asked Laura in a low tone.

"What do you mean?" Laura sat up and looked in the backseat.

"She sleeps long—her and the baby."

"I suppose she's just tired. She always looks after others, myself included. And the care of a baby with as much energy as that one can be quite demanding."

"And her eye? I've seen my share of black eyes—that's one of them." They were quiet. "So, tell me. Someone whoopin' on her?"

"If there was, there isn't any longer." Laura turned to look from the car's window, a hint of her desire to conclude the discussion.

Allan took note of the gage as he passed a small sign on the road, and soon pulled over for fuel. The Alabama filling station was surrounded by a wooded area. Two white men sat out front on large buckets. Allan put the car in park and stepped out. As he shoved the door closed behind him, he noticed black men and women who curiously marched into the trees, one-by-one, as though something was awry. He opened the car door and poked his head in to gain the attention of the ladies who waited inside.

"What do you think is going on out there?" he asked. Laura watched the people parade by. The white men on their buckets never raised an eyebrow in their direction, or bothered to glance.

"Whatever it is, it can't be good," Sophie said.

"What do you say we check it out?" Allan checked his pocket watch. "We have at least five hours of daylight. We're sure to make it to Georgia for the night by then."

"I suppose," Laura softly agreed. "Sure."

Allan climbed back into the car after he acquired the fuel, and drove alongside those who trekked down the newly formed dirt road. As they approached the center of the commotion, they noticed a sea of black faces; the crowd surrounded three charred bodies that hang from a white oak tree. The emerald leaves and thick branches casted shadows on the bodies of onlookers. Sophie immediately shielded her daughter's eyes from the grotesque visual of the lynched men. Slowly and silently, Laura and Allan exited the car.

Each step became increasingly heavier than the one before as Laura made her way through the multitude of black men, women, and children who mourned for those who dangled from the sturdy branch. Although the stench of burned flesh was repulsive, the scene was magnetic and drew from Laura a boldness she had yet to experience.

While two men attempted to cut the ropes and release the bodies from the tree, there was a woman who wailed loudly at the feet of one who hang; a second woman kneeled helplessly and stared at a second body suspended in air; and next to the third victim was a young boy. He was barely 8 years old; they called him Jessie. He was completely expressionless. He held a small twig in his hand and slowly broke it into pieces. He listened intently over the echo of the wailing woman for the low *crack* and *pop* each break would make, but it did not seem loud enough as he continued to snap the twig into small pieces until it was no more. He reached for another from the ground. Laura noticed, and approached him.

"Is this your papa?" she inquired. The boy nodded. Laura examined the hanging figure for a moment as Allan helped the other men release the bodies. Each of them cut at the ropes with pocket knives barely sharp enough for a steak.

"And where is your mama?" she asked the boy.

The boy shook his head and closed his eyes sullenly, and like the twig he snapped to pieces in his own hand, he crumbled—he broke apart without the utterance of a word or sound of despair. His expression was desperate and without solace. Laura rested her hand on the boy's shoulder, and sought the words to share with the inconsolable child. The two widows who wept amid the murdered were escorted away in preparation for the bodies to drop.

Laura spoke closely into the boy's ear. "Do not weep. The enemy has not won. *You*, my son, are still here." With that, she ushered the boy away from his father's lifeless, disfigured body. Hopelessly satisfied, the crowd dispersed, but Laura positioned herself to address them.

"No one will care more for their children than its mother—Africa," she spoke loudly. "And no one will protect and nurture the creation more than its Creator— God. This is not the time for fear. It is already done, and you can choose to fear no more. This is not the time for shame; the black blood that flows through every crevice of your being is strong, explosive, beautiful, and perfect. *You* should not live in fear. It is not your cross to bear. It is theirs. This—," she pointed to the bodies, "is the result of fear. Their fear of the power that you naturally possess. Hold your head up. You should be proud. Without cause, without a word, your light is so great that their only recourse is to dim it—and once you know pride—the pride of knowing the God who created you has made you perfectly productive beings—it is time to progress. It is time to do the work. It is time to connect to Mother Africa—to return home and to build communities for our brothers and sisters here that are thriving, resourceful and strong to bridge the gap. I've seen the north; you're no better there. Do not look for a way of escape when God has equipped you to excel. God is calling you to your rightful place in Him, and back home," she concluded and stepped away.

One by one, the bodies of the three men were released; they plummeted to the ground beneath them and sent up a bone-quivering thud.

Several approached to ask Laura her name and her purpose, or desired to know when and where they could hear more from her. She graciously entertained each of their questions before she returned to the waiting car. Allan lingered a while and discussed the tortured men with those who helped to cut them down from the tree. And after he overheard two ladies discuss Laura's brief message, he quickly made his way to the car for some UNIA flyers to better inform them.

Jessie, the young boy, stood near the car, eyes lowered and completely silent as Laura approached. She stooped slightly to the boy's ear, "Where are your kinfolks?"

He shook his head. Laura scanned the crowd, but when her search didn't point her in the direction of someone who would claim the boy, she stopped a woman as she passed.

"Is there anything you can tell me about the boy?" Laura pointed towards him.

"That's Jessie. One of those men was his daddy—we called him Lloyd. Poor boy. His mama died of pneumonia before he and his daddy came here a few months ago," the woman said.

Laura rested her hand on Jessie's shoulder. "Does he have any other family?"

"Not in these parts if he does."

The woman walked away and left Laura to make sense of the circumstances. She glanced to the backseat of the car where Sophie and Rachel, already seated inside, had left a small gap.

"Would you come with me?" she asked Jessie. He radiated in agreement—eyes wide and hopeful.

Laura opened the door and the boy climbed inside. Allan noticed from a distance, but he continued to distribute flyers to those who remained. He continued to lock eyes with Laura, so she shrugged hopelessly at his questioning stare, and waited inside the vehicle to continue their journey.

# CHAPTER
# SIX

The tribe walked in the front door of Allan's Jacksonville abode, a two-bedroom shotgun house. The curtains were drawn tightly, and not even a speck of light could enter the room. There was a musty odor, and the group fanned their hands quickly to escape the smell. Allan rushed over to the windows.

"I haven't been here for months," he said. "Let's get some air in here." Allan opened the curtains and windows, and as light entered the space, it exposed the mess he also left behind. He noticed, and swiftly removed piles of clothing that rested on his coffee table and sofa. "I was in a hurry."

"This is a nice place you have, Allan." Laura was polite. "And the people near here seem quite nice, hardworking."

Allan spoke proudly, "This area is called Hansontown. We're a bit north of where everything is, but the people around here are indeed hardworking people. They mean well." He looked at the sofa, recently cleared of laundry. "I'll sleep here. I also have a little cot, so Jessie can join me out here. There are two bedrooms down that hallway there. There are beds in each of them. But if you don't mind, just let me make sure it's clean for you ladies."

Sophie moved further into the room. "Take the time yah need." She went to the pantry hastily; there was nothing in it to eat. When she opened the ice box, a foul odor escaped into the room, and she closed it quickly. "I'll just take Rachel down tuh find a grocer."

"Mark's Foods is just a block over. They should have everything you need there."

"I'll come back wit' enough fuh everybody," Sophie said.

Laura dug into her handbag, and as Sophie walked past, she secretly handed her a few folded dollar bills.

Sophie shook her head defiantly, and said in a whisper, "No, Ms. Laura. I can't take yah money."

"And how do you expect to eat? Save whatever money you have." Laura clasped hands with Sophie as she buried the bills within her fists.

Sophie's eyes glistened—overcome with humility and gratitude for Laura's kind gesture.

"Hold your head up. This isn't pity. If you would like, you can work for me."

Sophie nodded and smiled. "Yes! Yes ma'am, I will."

"Then I owe you this, plus this week's pay. We'll talk about it later. But first," Laura moved closer to Sophie, "tell me, what were Jack's words? To see you go, and all?"

"He had left wit' some friends who come fuh 'em. I didn't say goodbye—just got what I could, and my baby, and was gone."

Laura did not know what to make of the runaway, but she was confident Sophie would be fine. "All will work out, and you and Rachel will have nothing to trouble yourselves over." Laura smiled. Sophie released a deep sigh and was comforted.

"Okay everybody," Sophie announced, "I'll be back as soon as I can tuh get dinner started." She left.

Laura inhaled deeply and looked to Jessie who stood in silence. She pondered the tone and pitch of his voice—if it were pleasantly sweet, or a bit raspy—and then wondered if he could speak at all. Space and time was the grace needed to coax him to a place of healing, so she gave it abundantly and refused to bother him with her own words, but kindly offered to be an ear whenever he desired to speak.

Allan walked towards a short hallway that led to two bedrooms, and then summoned Laura to follow.

"You can sleep here. The other room will be Sophie's for now," he said as he plopped the single bed pillow against his knee.

"Thank you."

"The pleasure's all mine, Ms. Laura. I know you all don't want to stay cramped up in here with me too long." He paused, and hoped she would playfully disagree. Laura said nothing. "I would like to take you around the city and show you a few things. It would be good to make Jacksonville your home."

"We'll see how peace leads." Laura tiptoed around the room and stopped to manipulate a framed image of an elderly woman who sat in a rocking chair. "How long have you been here?"

"Joined the UNIA Miami Division after prison about six years ago. Joined the Universal African Legion soon after."

"What is it that you do with them?" She blew dust from the frame.

"Military training and discipline—they teach us to protect our own."

"To fight?"

"No. The focus of the UNIA is community and a sustainable black economy. The Legion ensures nothing hinders them from doing that. Our goal isn't to create a stir, but to defend the organization, and the businesses we're raising up, against any attack from the outside."

"Oh, I see." Laura sat on the bed; it squeaked and drew attention away from the conversation.

"Chicago—where we met—needed reinforcement after a mob of white men vandalized a pharmacy owned by a UNIA officer. There are plenty already up there who can handle it, but whenever there is disruption, we all must be on guard and ready to protect what we've built. I've learned that when people take ownership of something, they take better care of it—become loyal."

"So, you were up there all that time—since we first met?"

Allan cleared the contents of a chest that rested at the foot of the bed, and piled his belongings near the door. "Yes. For as long as it took. Peace on a single day does not indicate what is to come. All it takes is someone looking at someone else the wrong way before the spark ignites into a full-blown flame. And with Garvey in prison, some may think we've weakened, and may try to attack at this point, but they're mistaken."

"I see," Laura said, pleased with the level of support and protection the program offered its people.

"There are several new constructions here in Jacksonville built by black hands. Not a strong UNIA presence, but that's why I'm here. I've been commissioned to increase UNIA membership in this city—help build enterprises that will employ blacks—and then protect it."

"Why is it that people need a membership to do what's already in their hearts to do—and especially the able-bodied?"

Allan leaned against the door frame and folded his arms across his chest. "The UNIA gives them a sense of community. We build together, we protect together, we grow together. When we all work on a single goal, we build it on a stronger foundation. The white man lumps all of us into one category—unwanted. Those who decide to divide and pursue without backing and support soon find destruction, or a business that's too weak to carry them too far."

Laura stood and walked over to a small window. She

pressed her palms against both sides of the frame and attempted to lift. It didn't budge, so Allan moved quickly to assist her.

"Let me help you with that." One of his hands gently swept across hers, and she backed away from him. She watched from a more suitable distance as he struggled to open the window. After a moment, a breeze hastily saturated the bedroom. "There."

"Thank you." She inhaled.

Allan dusted his hands together and then wiped them on his pants. "Let's say, after dinner this evening we all go downtown and I show you around."

"That will be fine." Laura pulled a slip of paper from her luggage and read it. "Tomorrow is the start of revival." She looked at Allan. "I've been asked to participate. This weekend, I will travel to Tampa by train. And then there is St. Petersburg the week after."

"You're already a busy woman." He smiled.

"Seems as if I'll be travelling and speaking each week for the next month. Arrangements made by those I've encountered in the north. I was not expecting so much so soon," she sighed deeply and placed the paper on the bed, "but God is consistent, and faithful."

"Is there anything I can do to help you?"

"You've done plenty. I'll rest a while until Sophie returns."

"I'll leave you to it, Ms. Laura." A thought hit him. "One more thing." He kneeled and reached beneath the bed. From the dark, hidden space, he drew out a rifle. "I don't know how familiar you may be with rifles, but this one here is mine. I may not always be around—I get called to one place or another and I will have to leave. Don't you forget where I put her." He stroked the weapon as though it were a good friend and slid it back beneath the bed.

Allan walked out, sure to grab his belongings piled at the door, and gave Laura the privacy she had silently requested.

~

The waters of the St. John's River crashed against the bank as Laura stood and observed the men who labored in the foreground. Small and medium-sized vessels docked periodically, and men, some young enough to be considered boys, would unload the boats and place freight onto the docks. It was near quitting time, but it seemed to not come fast enough for the men whose sweat was dried by the river's breeze before it could sting their eyes.

Children played near shallow ditches, emptied to lay water pipes. Laura resisted her urge to *shoo* the children who ran wildly, but stopped short—Rachel and Jessie were also intrigued by the makeshift play space.

"It must be a danger for them to play here," Laura said.

Sophie called for Rachel and Jessie, and then went to collect them.

"It probably won't do them any harm," Allan offered. "The city built playgrounds for the kids to play, but you won't find any of them in our parts."

Laura's face was tense, and wrinkled in places as she grew increasingly concerned for the playful children.

"Let's take the next trolley back up through the city," Allan continued. "There are a few things I would like to show you."

The crew loaded the rear of a streetcar that travelled north of the river. They passed a construction site where the workers had gone home, but the building, immaculate and beautiful, lured gawks from the city's new inhabitants. The side of the structure displayed the new Florida Theatre insignia, and each of their eyes widened. Within a moment's time, they passed another building that towered over all the others.

Allan explained, "This is the Barnett National Bank building. They put it up a few months ago—all 18 stories. I've never been inside, but it's a big one. Truth be told, about 25 years ago—I wasn't living here then—but a factory caught fire and a lot of the city burned down. Nearly 2,000 buildings gone in a matter of hours."

"Catastrophic." Laura added.

"It left a lot of people homeless. The city has been building bigger and better since. Every year it seems there is a new structure of some sort being put up."

"Looks tuh be plenty goin' on round heah," Sophie said. "Reminds me a lot of being back home."

"They may look similar, but you'll find the people in the south to be a little different." Allan checked his pocket watch. "It's time to get these young people off to bed. I have a meeting late this evening, and I want to be sure you all make it back in alright."

"Yes, sir," Sophie said playfully and wrapped her arm snuggly around Rachel who continued to peer at the gigantic structures. "I can't wait 'til mornin'. Wanna do a lil' explorin' of my own." She locked eyes with Laura. "I can take the children wit' me, of course, so yah can rest and prepare fuh service."

"They're no bother. God will give me all I need for tomorrow. Go. Get a good feel for this place." She smiled. "We may be here a while."

"Good then. I came across a woman in the store earlier who spoke of a nursin' school at a place called Brewster. One fuh black folks." She spoke hesitantly, "Thinkin' I'd take myself down there and apply."

"And without delay," Laura added.

That evening passed like many others. The five of them banded together—unified by one woman's quest to fulfill her mission.

# CHAPTER
# SEVEN

may 29^th 1927

Jacksonville welcomed Laura and her progressive talks. Each time she spoke, she gathered, at the very least, three dozen new members for the UNIA roster, and would be invited to speak in additional arenas near and far. She spoke of the power of the UNIA—how they had built sustainable communities, and how a greater part of their mission included an established barter system with her native Africa. Days of rest, which were few, found her engulfed in the solitude of the riverbanks. There, she was replenished and equipped with the peace to continue her journey, which quickly led her to Miami.

The warmth of proactive, black men and women resonated within the small lobby of the UNIA Miami Beach Headquarters. Various passersby greeted Allan as he escorted Laura down the corridor before they finally arrived at Claude Green's office. The president of the division,

Claude, was already engaged in conversation with two other men—Maxwell Cook, the southern branch captain, and Allan's good friend, James Nimmo, the colonel of legions.

Claude stood to greet the duo. "Come on in!" he said, excitement rolled from his tongue.

James noticed his friend as he entered and immediately stood to greet him, but Maxwell, tense and without a speck of regard, remained in his seat.

James and Allan hugged tightly and grinned without reservation. "Long time. How was the north?" James asked, and delivered a single pat on Allan's back.

"Same filth, different dirt," Allan responded passively. He walked over to greet Claude.

"Glad to have you back, brother," Claude said, and hugged Allan tightly.

"It's good to be back, but more importantly, it's good to have an extra hand on deck."

James took a step in Laura's direction, and pleasantly extended his hand to her, but did not say a word; he waited for her to finally utter something amongst the men in the room, but she said nothing. She returned his gesture with a firm handshake and a subtle nod of her head, laced with an amiable smile.

Claude briefly examined the woman who stood tall in the shadow of the doorway. "And you must be Ms. Kofi, our sister from Africa." He approached, grasped her hand, and continued to speak as he gently released it from his firm grip. "You've lit numerous fires in the north. I hope you don't plan to take pause down here in the south."

Laura smiled. "The contrary."

Allan offered, "She has been working nearly every night since we've been in Florida."

James said, "Really? I heard that the little lady here hasn't been wished well by many pastors up north, and even a few down here."

"Clears their congregations right on out when she's in town," Claude contributed with a chuckle.

Maxwell finally stirred in his chair. He looked to Allan and purposely avoided Laura, whose attention he seemed to have at that moment. "Preachers? The UNIA rests on a solid foundation of hard work, skill, and promotes the progress of the Negro people. We are beyond a measly faith-based organization. There are others out there."

Allan spoke in Laura's defense. "That's not what this is, brother."

"History hasn't proven the church to be effective at releasing black folks from bondage—physically or mentally—to get equality or sufficient housing, care, or goods for our families," he lectured. "It is the UNIA's duty to focus more on a united front of able-bodied people who can stand in defense of all that is right, and for what we are entitled to, than to take to their knees—begging."

"I've spoken to Garvey," Allan interjected. "And he wants her on board. She can be useful. I've seen this woman speak to crowds of thousands, and it seems every single one would leave more empowered than they walked in. Not to mention, the nearly 50 new memberships each time she's spoken in halls and gatherings down here in the south."

Claude added, "Let's not forget, Maxwell, the church is at the center of every organizing effort for blacks. So, Allan here has a point." He spoke directly to Laura, "Garvey insists he meets with you soon, so I'm planning to send several of you on a train up to Atlanta as early as the end of the month, but I would like to see you in action. So, tell us, how do you expect to impact the people here in Miami?"

She responded, "The bigger picture, a commercial shipping line for direct trade with Africa. The easier feat, a community of self-sufficient blacks." Laura looked pointedly at Maxwell. "And all in the name of God."

Maxwell's eyes burned through Laura's soul; it was impossible to conceal his disgust. "I'm sure there is a need for you with the Black Cross Nurses. You might want to consider it."

"No, thank you," Laura responded with a raised brow.

The men expected more of a roar from Laura, but she merely thanked each of the gentlemen in the room for meeting their acquaintance, and walked out as pleasantly as she had entered; she knew any further interaction with Maxwell would be unfruitful.

On their hasty walk down the crowded block of retail stores and small restaurants, there was awkward silence until Allan mustered the words to break it. "You have plenty to offer this organization. Don't ever think differently."

"It is not the organization that I was created to serve, but God, so I do not seek their validations; nor do I seek any value they place upon me. I have a thorough understanding of my own worth."

"And Maxwell, he doesn't really mean—."

Laura interjected, "There is no need to explain his character. It is clear."

Impressed, Allan smirked. "You're not like many women I've encountered. You don't need things explained to you, or help, or to feel secure."

Laura secured her feet against the concrete and took pause. "That is where you're wrong. I have insecurities that run as deep as the Nile; I need help most days, and I constantly seek understanding. I've simply learned a long time ago that man can give me none of those things. They can only speak to my ego, but never create any real change." The two continued at a slower pace.

"I see you have it all figured out."

"No, but I know the One who does."

Allan was quiet, unaware of how to address her response.

"So, tell me this: what are your plans here in America? When do you think you'll return to Africa?" he furthered the conversation.

"How, or when, or if I'll ever return is not up to me, but the One who sent me."

Again, Allan was stumped, and failed to know how to address Laura's consistent references to the Spirit Being.

Although he had childhood memories of Sunday School with his grandmother, those days were long behind him. It seemed to him that Laura spoke a language in which he was not well versed.

"It's quite bold of you." He reflected on the level of submission and sacrifice Laura consistently enacted. "You must be afraid."

"Yes, but not more than before I came here. I did not want to come." Laura chuckled to herself. "I heard His call some time before, and I ran."

"Ran? Like Jonah?" Allan grabbed hold of a bit of confidence as a rare childhood memory flooded back into his thoughts.

Laura smiled and locked eyes with him. "You know the Word a little, I see." Allan smirked. "But yes, I ran. For a season, God allowed me to become ill. It was when I believed I would die that I agreed to journey here. And then I was made well. So, you see, I fear less being here than what I would face if I were not."

"So, there is no prince back in Africa waiting for your return?"

Laura giggled at the thought. "Yes, but the prince is my brother."

Allan laughed. "You know what I mean."

"I was never married. I spoke of it before."

"Just wanted to be sure." He pressed his lips together and scratched his head. "There is a UNIA fund-raiser ball being held next week. Would you like to accompany me?"

"I cannot say I have ever attended such an event."

"Well, there's a first time for everything."

~

The women of the UNIA postured themselves as a more poised replica of their male counterpart—organized, intelligent, and determined to conquer whatever may be placed before them—but only under the strict rule of the men. Most of them took on the roles of nurses and educators within the UNIA. They met separately from the men, created pamphlets and manuals that outlined proper hygiene, safety, and emergency procedures. They prayed often, and more often than that, they cared for the children who would grow up to be business leaders or members of the legion.

The sun was nearly settled on the horizon when Laura walked into the women's meeting. Allan wanted to ensure she found her way, so he escorted Laura into the building. He stopped for a moment to greet a few other brothers who waited at the door—a deterrent for any mischievousness or altercations that could arise, especially by officers of the law who showed on occasion to intimidate UNIA leaders and members.

Over seventy women were spread across a small community room. Some of them wore nurses' uniforms, and others dressed in ankle-length skirts and blouses. The children were corralled in another room in the back of the building as the women found their chairs.

"Take your seats now," the leader, a woman of light complexion and a slightly crooked smile, spoke. "We have a few affairs to discuss before we can close this evening. Let's be mindful of the hour."

After he concluded his conversation, Allan entered in time to find Laura a seat near the front. He led her there— which emphasized her importance and position in the absence of a formal introduction. The women followed her with their eyes until she was seated, but the leader's eyes remained hopelessly locked on Allan—even as he left the room. Once he was out of sight, she gazed at Laura before she continued.

"First, let's begin with prayer," she said. The women stood and, as they were led, each of them began to mumble, chant, whisper, or exalt. The moment was not theirs, but for the One who gathered them together again. When the women's foreheads glistened in the warmth of the room—

because they were gathered so closely—a few wiped away tears that streamed loosely, and they took their seats.

"I am grateful that each of you are here today," the leader continued. "For those who are not familiar, I am Carmen Philips, Matron of the Miami Branch Black Cross. This is Sharon Tealey," she gestured towards the woman who sat at her left, "our secretary. And next to her is Mary Roberts, our Head Nurse."

The women offered a brief applause before Carmen continued, "Let's begin tonight's discussion on the topic of education. We must all learn to thoroughly read and write. Raise your hand if you can do neither of those things." Several hands went into the air. "It is impossible to help explain healthy practices to the community and guide them through all of the leaflets we've created as reminders for them if we don't know how to read it ourselves. Now, there will be courses here three nights a week that will help those of you who aren't good readers and writers." She reached for a clipboard that had a few sheets of white paper attached and held it up. "I'm going to send this around the room. Be sure to write your name, and the name of any other woman in this community that could use the lessons."

The clipboard was passed around, and one by one women scribbled their names on the page. Laura made a mental note of the women who were uneducated; she followed the clipboard with her eyes from person to person until it would eventually cause her to rudely turn in her seat, so she returned her attention to the speaker.

"Secondly, we've heard your concerns about the plumbing in Colored Town. The water can make you sick if you don't boil it first, so don't drink it until you've done so. Don't give it to your babies, and don't advise anyone else to do it either."

A hand went up near the front of the room. The woman stood. "It's not just that. Water is one thing, but it's the sickness. There was about sixteen people sick last week—all living within walking distance from each other. They complain of pain and loose bowels. Is that the water? I don't think it is." The woman sat down again.

"We need better, more sanitary places to relieve ourselves. We're talking to the city officials, and we hope they will soon help to bring plumbing to Colored Town. Until then, the people there are in such proximity to each other that you must advise them to keep their hands and bodies as clean as possible—especially the children who touch their stool sometimes without knowing it—before putting anything near their mouths."

The evening continued as Carmen addressed safety and the children's education. Laura sat and listened intently. She made both mental and physical note of what plagued the women, and the commitments they had made to the community she also served.

When the final question was answered, and the women made their way to the door, Laura approached the front of the room where Carmen packed away leaflets she had brought to share with those in attendance.

"Good evening," Laura extended her hand. "My name is Laura—Kofi."

Carmen distrustfully returned the gesture and shook Laura's hand. "You sound like our brothers and sisters from Africa. Is that so?"

"Yes. Accra—the Gold Coast."

"Well, it's good to have you." Carmen flashed her crooked smile. "How long will you be here for? What's your cause?"

"Just this week, and then I'll travel back to north Florida. Before my time here expires, I will be speaking in Liberty Hall nightly. Will you be in attendance?"

Allan encroached upon the cordial ladies; he cleared his throat with a sharp *eh-hem*. "Are you ready to set out to the hotel? It's best we leave here before late."

"Hello, Allan," Carmen said, smile faded into an abyss. "Nothing wrong with speaking. Right?"

"Good evening, Ms. Carmen," he rushed.

"So, you're taking care of Ms. Laura here, I see."

"As best I can." He turned his attention to Laura who witnessed the awkward dialogue between the two and could only attribute it to some failed romance. "Let's go."

Carmen added, "I know you'll take good care of her. That's what you do best. Only privileged women get to experience it. Consider yourself lucky, Ms. Laura." She grabbed her knapsack and roughly stuffed a few more papers inside. "Get her home," she said somberly.

Carmen's eyes had been opened to the possibilities of Allan's passionate acquaintance, but his lack of interest led her to claw for any opportunity to appeal to him. She found herself in Laura's meetings each night—an attempt to get a whiff of the scent Allan had picked up and was lured by. She was harmless, yet curious enough to watch their interactions from afar. Carmen's quest did not end as soon as she thought it would. Laura's week-long series gathered over 3,000 people and caused her to stay an additional week beyond what she assumed she would. And in that time, Laura gathered over 900 new UNIA members. Carmen was intoxicated by the essence that rested on Laura's life—and she made peace with it.

~

## august 1, 1927

In the weeks that followed the Miami conferences, Allan and Laura were led through a corridor of the Atlanta Prison by a white guard who was clad in uniform and toted a pistol on his waist band. With them for the train ride north were several other members of the UNIA who had all been anxious to meet the man waiting there—and included Maxwell, the source of Laura's greatest criticism. Only two people in the party were permitted to speak with the prisoner at a time. Allan and Laura were up first.

In an enclosed room at the end of the walkway, Marcus Garvey, dark and unkempt, was seated perfectly upright, hands folded, elbows nestled firmly on the table before him, and prepared to conduct business. Prison had far from stripped him of his cause, and he was as determined as ever.

The guard unlocked the bars. "He's in here. You have 15 minutes. No more." The two nodded in unison, and Allan led Laura to the man who waited at the table. Marcus stood, and the two men embraced.

In the sweet, Jamaican accent of his native island, Marcus spoke. "Brother," he said, and leaned back to have a look at him.

Allan smiled. "It's so good to see you."

"How good is it to see me here?"

"I can't say the visual is good, but your health is what matters at this point."

"The health of the body, what you can see, leaves a man first, but it is the health of his mind that many fail to notice. Death or health, what matters most is the forward movement of the UNIA and our cause."

Allan smirked, "And that is why I brought her here." Laura stepped from behind Allan. "This is Princess Laura Kofi from Africa's Gold Coast."

Laura extended her hand to Marcus. "It is a pleasure," he said as their hands united.

Laura spoke firmly, "Your cause is as alive as you are. It's been an honor to join it, and each of the men and women who fight restlessly for change—improvement. We have similar ambitions." She walked around the table and took a seat.

"Ambition?" Marcus asked as he sat. "It's not a word I heard often from the broken people I encountered outside of here."

"I am from another place. A place that has bred me to be a warrior in spirit, in mind, and in action. I am not tainted by brokenness and inferiority—branded by slavery."

"Oh, I see. Your eyes have no filter."

"Filter?" she inquired.

"Yes. Count it a blessing. The Negro man and Negro woman cannot see themselves without filtering the image of who they truly are through what whites have told and shown them. You tell a black man that he's strong," Marcus clutched his fist, "and powerful, and his thoughts trickle back to the pain of the lash, or what he felt the moment he saw his uncle, father, or brother hanging from a tree. And he sees himself as inferior and weak. You tell the Negro woman that she is powerful, desirable, and worthy of being protected, and she filters it through years of rape, degradation, or of being handed over by a submissive Negro in fear of his life if he failed to comply. If you ever filter something as pure as clean water through dirt, you will always have a tainted visual. The amount of dirt will determine the thickness of the mud blinding your sight. Some people's visions have been cemented. It is my greatest task to chisel away at it for them to see, and most of them, for the very first time."

Laura digested every word. "My spiritual eye is what guides me, not the physical. Even without physical sight, I can still cling tightly to vision. My sight is as pure as God created it. My mission is to teach others to see spiritually, and to work physically."

"The only god many people around here know told them they were created to be enslaved, to belong to another man, to have no identity but the one of human property. It's branded into them, and their scars are constant reminders."

Allan interjected, "It is difficult to get our followers to desire more for themselves, to see their capabilities above their fears and shortcomings, to teach them who they are."

"You can't teach creation who they are if they have a crucial misconception of their Creator," Laura offered.

Marcus leaned in, and spoke equally with his hands. "We speak of God in our rallies and assemblies and publications, but we'll leave Christian education to the church. We have built a community, a society, of Negro people ready and able to do the work."

"I believe she can help with that. I've seen her pack out a building night after night, leaving people hanging on to every word, and they linger long after shut down for opportunities to do something more."

Marcus silently contemplated Allan's comments and then examined Laura searchingly with his eyes. "What is it that you want?"

Laura stared at him, and sought clarity for his question.

Marcus continued, "Is it fame? Money?"

Laura spoke without pause, "Both."

Bewildered, Allan inquired, "What?"

Marcus locked eyes with Allan disappointedly, and then sat back in his chair. Allan was lured to the corner of the room, appalled by Laura's response to the great leader's question, and fearful he had misjudged her intentions.

Laura explained. "I want fame, which will enable me to draw people to God's instruction. I want money to build a functioning trading system with Africa, one that will enable many here to emigrate there. I want both. I will not cut corners. God will dictate each step I take towards completing the work."

Allan relaxed his posture in the self-directed time-out as his concern subsided.

Marcus sat up and leaned in to Laura who sat directly across from him. "How would you like to officially become the new National Field Representative for the UNIA?" he asked.

From the corner of the room, Allan smiled, satisfied.

# CHAPTER
# EIGHT

In a dimly lit ballroom, over a hundred blacks dressed in their finest attire were engaged in conversation, or danced to the up-tempo jazz rhythms of the live band, or secretly partook in alcohol. Sweat beaded pleasantly on the exposed bosoms of the dancing ladies; the men perspired less gracefully in their collared shirts and created oval rings beneath their arms. The heat was immense, and nearly unbearable near those whose energy lit the night; they laughed loudly, and threw their bodies around majestically as though consumed by the tunes.

A different side of Allan was awakened by the night's festivities. A youthful energy radiated from each of his movements—slow and confident. He greeted familiar faces and pressed his way through the crowd before he spotted a group of fellow leaders.

"There are a few people you should meet," he said to Laura, and then smiled at a few party-goers who passed behind her.

In a section farthest from the band, Laura was introduced to several leaders of the UNIA who spoke highly of her recent engagements, which packed out Liberty Hall night after night—and even those who were present at several lectures and sermons in Tampa. After introductions and various pleasantries, Laura revisited her overwhelming apprehension to become completely comfortable. She nudged Allan slightly as he whistled to the sound of the trumpet.

Laura asked, "So, what is the benefit of this occasion?" Laura stretched herself to find something amusing, but failed when she noticed the cash box at the door that overflowed with money collected from party-goers, the drunkenness of those around her, and an exhilarating lifestyle contradictory to the one she lived.

He permitted her intrusion, and raised his voice to speak over the trumpet's blare. "We raise money for our efforts. And we show the community a good time while we do it."

"And there's been progress?" Laura inquired as she leaned in a little closer so that he would hear her clearly. She could not understand the nature of the celebration, so she proceeded with as much caution as any woman beyond her element would.

Allan spoke cautiously, and gathered his thoughts as he went. "We're still shifting some mindsets that are stuck in the old slave ways, but we're raising the money to fund the cause."

"You're raising the money to keep them enslaved." Laura's words were the fists that struck his belly with much intensity.

Allan teetered on bewilderment and offence. "Slaves?"

She pointed towards the people who partied, drunk and exhausted, on the dance floor. "Here. These people are no freer than the day the trumpet sounded to release them. And this program is profiting from their temporary escape from their issues. Prayer meetings, consecration—those are the tools that will destroy the damage created in their masters' houses, and it will propel a powerful army of black men and women to produce and to grow—not dance. Why celebrate when you have yet to win?"

After he partly digested her words, "If you'd like to go, Ms. Laura, I don't mind taking you home." Allan did not understand fully, but he wanted to comply with her wishes—even if it meant their departure.

"I think I've seen my share. If you don't mind."

Laura turned to exit in the manner she had come when she unexpectedly came face to face with Carmen, whose sparkling, black garment arose slightly above the knee and accentuated every curve of her tall frame. Her red lips distracted from her crooked smile.

"Hey there, Ms. Laura." Her speech was slurred and a small splotch of red was smeared across both of her front teeth. She looked to Allan and widened her eyes as pleasantly as she could. "Leaving so soon?" she whined.

"It's late, and we must be going," Laura responded.

"*We?*" The alcohol had given Carmen confidence to pry. "If I weren't mistaken, I would say you two are an item." She feigned laughter. "Well, is it so?"

"It is not," Laura answered.

"Well, be careful. The ladies around here like to call this one *Slick*." She poked at Allan's chest.

"That's enough, Carmen," Allan interfered.

"What? Just some friendly conversation." And to Laura, "You know, us women got to stick together. Would hate to see the ruin of a beautiful spirit such as yours."

Laura pacified her with a gentle pat on the back and moved past her. To Laura, any quarrel over a man was for girls, and *sh*e was a woman—one who could not be tempted to lose herself for such trivial things. The cost of her journey had been too great.

Allan locked eyes with Carmen and shook his head as he walked away; Carmen examined herself for a moment, and then was lost again in the crowd.

~

The next evening, in a packed, Miami church, Laura spoke from the pulpit of a reverend who had heard of her appeal to the masses. Despite the thunderstorm, which typically kept people inside, they arrived in droves, and drenched from their commute. They listened attentively to her message.

"Your body is free, but your soul is in bondage. You're possessed even when you're free. I visited New York City. Men and women line up each night to serve in a venue that will never serve them—where they will neither eat nor drink in the presence of its white clientele—where they make a mockery of you and your ancestor's suffrage by re-creating the atmosphere that made them superior. The Cotton Club. They've seen more than their share of cotton yet they still *pick* it as their big break, their opportunity, their progress. You are not unlike them. You imprison the gifting of God—you sing, and dance, and play for a people who are more entertained by your servitude than your performance. And when that is not enough, you sing and dance to forget your worries, your hardships. Never forget it. Take it to the Master instead, and allow Him to mold it into something greater, and for His use. You are kings and queens. Never forget."

As her speech ended, a collection plate was passed—stacked high with money. Unbeknownst to Laura, two UNIA officials, a man and woman dressed in dark clothing, sat quietly in her meeting that evening. They listened intently, and took note of the money that was collected. Neither of them approached Laura to announce their presence, but they met secretly beyond her view after they observed the overflow of foldable currency.

Lightening flashed at a slower rate than when they had arrived when the service finally ended. A small group of parishioners remained to consult with Laura.

"I just wanted to say how grateful I am that you came here tonight, Sister Kofi." A middle-aged man, bald and handsome, initiated the conversation. "I built a little store that carried food and goods. Was open for nearly a month, when the white man from 3 blocks away comes by and says I have to close—that his customers, black folks, weren't coming to shop with him anymore."

"I see." Laura leaned in. Exhausted from her frequent engagements, she gestured for them to sit and talk while she rested from her feet.

"See, the negroes couldn't even step foot in his store. They would be served from a little window in the back of the shop. They weren't allowed in—and then I put up a store they could step foot in. And then—," his emotions were a tsunami ready to crash against the shore, "he burnt it down." His sobs made it difficult to decipher his words, but Laura did not seek clarification. Instead, she extended her hand, placed it on his back and prayed for him.

"I tried to do what was right," he continued when Laura quieted. "What could help my people—my family. It was all I had."

"You can rebuild," Laura insisted.

"Yeah," a woman who sat next to him added bitterly, "but they make it so hard for us to get what we need. Permit this, document that. They don't want us to use what they have for their own kind, but make it hard for us to do it for ours."

"There are programs that will both support and protect you." Laura reached into her bag and pulled out a flyer for the UNIA. "I've seen it with my own eyes. These are people who will create a thriving black economy. I know it. The work has already begun. You too can take part. Here, take."

They read over the document as Laura continued. "Not only that, we are preparing for a continuous African exodus—to return to the land from which you, and I, came."

The woman asked, "How do you plan to do that?"

"Ships. It is my mission to fund a sawmill that will help us to manufacture the vessels we'll need for travel. It's already underway."

"It won't be able to carry all of us there, will it?" the woman asked skeptically.

"It is my understanding that not all of you will want to go. My duty is to give you all the option, and the access to return home."

Before she allowed a drop of hope to rise within her and drench her agitation, the woman said, "We've never been there. How do we know what it's like?"

"I can only guarantee it is not like *this* place—filled with pain and lack. What would one have to lose to go to a place where they are embraced by those who look as they do? What is *here* that you must hold tightly to?"

"For one, I've known this place my whole life. Everybody I've ever known is here. And we have just as much of a right to be here as they do."

"And you are right," Laura added. "So, when are you going to tell *them* that? Stand up for yourselves? When will you stop being shoved around like a ragdoll?" The woman silently contemplated Laura's words. "The UNIA can help you just as much as you can help them."

The man and woman looked down at the leaflets again, and were calmed by a new sense of direction and possible solutions. And as she had done night after night, Laura had successfully enlightened them on the strength and ability of the UNIA. She believed in it as much as she believed in the God who sent her to serve alongside them. Some judged her refusal to be infected by the invisible plague of mediocrity and worthlessness, and her dissociation from worldly pleasures, which helped her to avoid distraction from her mission. In all, not a fraction of ill-intent could be scraped from the crevices of her heart, which was pure.

~

Laura kneeled beside her bed in prayer, the way she began each morning; she would steal away in the peace of barely lit skies. She whispered her offerings to God with caution to not disturb those who slept in nearby hotel rooms. Before she could finish, Laura's exultation was interrupted by Rachel's playful screams on the other side of the wall, and the faint sound of her mother's correction.

Sophie called out, "Stop it, gal! Hush all that screamin'. It's too early."

Laura's attempt to continue in prayer failed. Rachel's giggles were a consistent distraction. She concluded with an "amen" as Sophie slightly opened the door and peeked inside.

"Aww, Ms. Laura, I didn't mean fuh this gal to wake yah."

Laura arose from her knees. "It's fine, Sophie. I'm awake." Rachel bounced into the room and sat on Laura's bed.

"Get down from there, gal!" Sophie ordered.

"She's fine," Laura insisted.

Allan appeared in the doorway behind Sophie as he folded a blanket. "Well, I guess I'm up," he yawned.

The four of them offered morning salutations, and then looked to Jessie who was still sound asleep on a cot near Laura's bed. Concerned, she walked over and gently caressed his forehead. "Let him rest. This world has been harsh."

"But that can't be normal, Ms. Laura," Sophie said. "He sleeps, and don't talk much at all, just nods his head when yah ask 'em somethin'."

Laura continued to caress Jessie's face. "Let him be. He will speak when he has something meaningful to say."

# CHAPTER
# NINE

At the Miami UNIA headquarters one evening, Claude Green sat at his desk and shuffled through papers. He read one, placed it on the desk, and then picked up another. The phone rang. Very few others were in the building, but he was certain someone else was available to answer. He was right. Within moments, his assistant walked through the door.

"I'm sorry to interrupt, Mr. Green, but you have a call," she said.

"I'll take it here," Claude responded. He placed the papers he had thumbed through on the desk and picked up the phone as his assistant sauntered from the room. He cleared his throat. "This is Claude." He continued to speak as if he had been reunited with an old friend; he even flashed a smile at the sound of the voice on the other end. "Hey there. It's good to hear from you." He paused and smiled brighter. "Things are going well here."

Claude listened to the caller and pressed the phone

tightly to his ear. "Oh, you heard about that? Yeah, the little lady is a trailblazer," he exclaimed.

He listened further, and then shifted the phone from one ear to the other. His smile dimmed completely as he sat high in his chair—shoulders stiff and tense. His lips parted as he listened closely to the other end of the line.

"Oh? No, we have carefully monitored the collection of every dollar taken in at each of her events. So, it is impossible for her to have spent—." He silenced himself. "Please, just give me time to consider this further." He listened for a while longer.

"Don't be concerned. All is taken care of on this end. You take care of yourself in there." Claude hung up the phone and then slouched back in his chair, overwhelmed by the news he received.

~

At Liberty Hall, Laura stood behind a podium, hair pinned tightly from her face; her skin glistened as the humid room caused her to delicately perspire. She concluded a message to a packed house of attendees with as much zeal as she could muster.

"Negroes, learn to help yourselves, create your own jobs, build your own enterprises. Clean up your lives—love one another, patronize one another's storehouses, lunch counters, and services. If you don't learn to help yourselves and build industries and commerce with your Motherland Africa, you are doomed and done for. Don't send preachers to Africa who know nothing else to do but preach. Send dedicated and God-fearing men and women skilled in trades and qualified in professions. Let's ready ourselves for what is to come and refuse to look back on what was. Let's begin now."

An applause rang out as she walked away from the podium. Allan waited near the platform for her to step down. Four men carried a collection plate in each hand and passed them down every row. Many dropped coins inside the vessels, and others dropped a single bill until each of them arrived at the front of the room and were picked up.

With Allan close at her side, Laura made her way to a small meeting room at the back of the facility. Claude was there along with two other leaders of the Miami region UNIA—including Maxwell, who sat at the table in the center of the room, and whose disgust was always incredibly difficult to conceal.

"What a pleasure to see you here, Mr. Green," Laura started. She was followed into the room by a single attendant who carried the stacked containers of money. He placed it on the table and immediately exited.

Claude stared boldly at Laura. "I see you've done well, Ms. Laura."

"Well enough to steal money from the organization that feeds you, huh?" Maxwell accused.

Passively, Laura said, "First, there is no organization that feeds me. Second, I have stolen nothing."

"That's not what we've heard. In the past two months, you've spoken in the name of the UNIA, have accounted for over $12,000, but we hear you have set some aside for yourself," Maxwell said.

"I have done no such thing," Laura denied.

Claude gently approached Laura. "So, you haven't raised funds to be used outside of UNIA causes and purposes?"

"No."

"The sawmill being built—," Maxwell volunteered.

"What of it?" she asked sharply.

"All with your own personal money?" Maxwell continued.

Allan locked eyes with Maxwell, and resisted the urge to interfere with their discussion, but as the interrogation intensified, it became an unbearable challenge.

"Our mission is to create trade with Africa. We must establish industry here in America to do so. The sawmill is necessary to build the ships for transport—and travel. Not only does it employ black people, and equip them with industry skills, they will work diligently to prepare the vessels we need."

Curious, Claude inquired, "And who approved this expense?"

"I did," Laura spoke firmly.

"You have no authority," Maxwell piped up.

"I have *all* authority," Laura retorted.

"Let me handle this, Maxwell," Claude said.

Laura lifted her head boldly. "I need not the approval of man to do what God has called me to do."

"Are you serious? God? Step out of the clouds and cough up the money you've taken." Maxwell did not mask his thoughts.

Claude moved closer to Laura and spoke compassionately. "Garvey must hear of this. Unauthorized purchases and misuse of UNIA funds is a major offense."

Maxwell angrily jumped from his seat. "This bitch *steals* from us and that's all she gets?"

Without a moment of thought or restraint, Allan physically jumped to Laura's defense and pounced on Maxwell. Startled, Laura shifted towards the door as the two men shoved each other, which soon caused Maxwell to pick himself up from the floor; but it was not all Allan's fault. Maxwell stumbled over a chair and his foot had been caught in an instant.

"That's enough!" Claude yelled.

"You know where to find me," Allan panted as Maxwell got to his feet. Claude and a second man held Allan at his shoulders.

A third man stood face to face with Maxwell and attempted to block his movement.

Maxwell laughed, "I see money isn't the only thing she has her little paws on." He straightened the collar of his shirt, and re-tucked the tail end into his pants. "Allan must be having that little itch scratched by the little princess here.

So, how is it, Allan?" He grabbed his crotch. "You know, royal coochie?"

"Son of a bitch!" With as much strength as he could muster, Allan attempted to push beyond the two men who held him back from further attack on Maxwell. He continued to struggle against the restraint.

"That's right! Show her who you really are. Following around this little church mouse like you're holy when we're from the same gutter. Let's not forget, you're the one with the record to prove it." Maxwell laughed nervously.

Allan noticed Laura, who watched from the doorway, and he calmed himself. The veins that had risen to the surface at his anger began to ease.

Maxwell shoved past the man who remained in his way and prevented the violent acts he imagined. "Get the hell on." Without another word, Maxwell left the room abruptly.

Finally released from the human chains, Allan gripped the back of a chair, lifted it and slammed it into the floor, a final release before he attempted to completely regain his composure. He slowed his breath with a few deep exhales, and then looked over to Laura who stood puzzled—her hand pressed firmly against her chest.

"Are you okay, Ms. Laura?" Allan asked.

Laura gave him a stern once-over with piercing eyes, and then left his presence without a response. Allan felt the heaviness of her reaction and hang his head.

~

With a new dawn, Laura sat on the small, wooden porch of the lodge and sipped a cup of tea as she watched Jessie angrily hit at a tree with a stick. He would not relent, but since it hurt no one, Laura never thought to stop the behavior.

The screen door creaked open, and there was a slight shuffle. Allan cautiously walked onto the porch. He first noticed the boy who awkwardly *whooped* a tree, but when he saw Laura, he stopped to gather his thoughts before he approached.

"Is he still not talking?" he inquired as he continued to stare at the spectacle.

"He's talking. Just not how one would expect. *This* is how he expresses pain." Laura stared straight ahead.

Allan continued to probe. "And you believe the boy should be acting like this? Doesn't seem normal to me."

"What?" She looked at Allan inquisitively. "Hitting things?"

"I'm sorry. I didn't know how else to—."

"Then you do nothing. How are people supposed to understand my cause with you consistently coming to my aid? My intentions are muddled by your imposing bravery," Laura spoke sternly.

"And who else is there to help you? To protect you?"

"God is—."

"God is a lot of things, but He can't be made accountable for your stubborn unwillingness to recognize you need—you need me."

"Need *you*? I don't need anyone but—."

"God?" Allan shook his head, and turned to walk back inside, but he stopped short of the threshold. "You ever think God could send a *man* to protect you? Perhaps you should get off your high horse and climb back down to earth. God *does* cause people in the natural to do the things He, as a spirit, cannot physically do. I guess that's the one lesson you've conveniently missed in all your learning."

Allan walked back inside, and Laura, unaffected, returned her gaze to the exhausted boy who sat near the tree. Jessie had grown tired of his aggressive swats.

A sip of tea later, Laura observed Rachel as she sprang from the door and playfully ran over to Jessie. Once Rachel noticed his condition, she gracefully placed her hand on his shoulder. Jessie locked eyes with her in quiet understanding. The example in front of her had been made clear, and Laura sighed in her acceptance of clarity.

# CHAPTER TEN

The dust had not settled on the altercation that surrounded her alleged theft of UNIA funds, yet Laura found herself at the helm of a rally and spoke to a crowd of discouraged, black laborers, and their families, who had recently lost their jobs. In Allan's absence, whose presence created more contention than support, Sophie stood nearby.

"Many blacks are clawing to get north, but north is not the answer," Laura bellowed. "To be willing to settle in a place where there is *less* killing is settling *for* less. East should be our goal—we should sail the Atlantic until we reach a new coast. Let us not stop until we get there. We will create our own jobs, and trade with our own people until we all reach the Mother Land."

The crowd cheered. A woman, small in stature, walked through the crowd and distributed copies of a newsletter.

She was barely seen as she moved, but she left a path of periodicals that were slightly raised into the air as people read them. Laura noticed, but did not allow the stranger's actions to deter her from her most important points. Eventually, the cheers turned to chatter and the rally was completely disrupted.

Sophie walked into the crowd and grabbed a copy of the publication; she snatched one directly from the hand of the female intruder. The cover of the *Negro World* revealed an image of Laura during a speaking engagement; the words "SHE'S A FAKE" were sprawled across the top.

A few in the crowd slowly dispersed as they read the interior, but many of them remained and placed it aside. Laura soon yielded to the commotion, and signaled to Sophie who slowly approached. Sophie's eyes moved as quickly as they could through each written line of the article. She opened the publication to its most crucial content to reveal the cause of the disorder to Laura.

~

As evening fell, Laura's initial outrage had softened to sheer annoyance. She paced the floor of her hotel room, and held a copy of the *Negro World* in her hand. There was a knock at the door.

"Come in," she said, disgruntled.

Allan entered the room. He first desired to take the pulse of the atmosphere before he spoke—caution afforded to him by his recent run-in with her.

"I assume you've read this too?" she asked. "A fake?" She threw the paper onto the bed. "It says I was born in Georgia. It says I am a thief, and the UNIA has dissociated from me. Anything to discredit me and to weaken my following." She plopped down on the bed. "And I've called the UNIA office, several of them, and none will return my calls."

For the first time, Allan heard Laura refer to herself and

*her* followers when she spoke of her God-ordained mission. Frustration, fear, and embarrassment had altered her perception.

"You must be careful, Laura," Allan finally spoke after he was certain she had released all she desired to say. "I know how this works. You've upset some really powerful people down here."

"Powerful? Tuh!"

"Don't underestimate them. They may be black, but they're powerful enough."

"To do what?"

"I can't say for sure. I just think now is a good time to lay low for a while. Maybe we can head back to Jacksonville—just for a season."

"God's work isn't finished here," she insisted, and then buried her face in her hands.

"But *your* work just may be. Laura, listen, you don't want to—."

"Who are you to tell me what is to be done?" She stood with great hostility. "Be it that I am a woman you should demand that I rest, that I flee, that I hide? If I were a man, would you say such things? Would you see me as fragile, in need of protection? I am in need of no one but Almighty God."

Allan backed away and placed his open palms in front of his body—a moment of surrender. "Then there is nothing to be said. You've made up your mind."

He began to walk out of the room when he doubled back, and left the door slightly open. Allan rushed over and stood face to face with Laura. "No," he spoke with authority. "There is plenty to say, but you won't live to hear it if you stay here."

"I will live just fine." She refused to back down.

He spoke passionately. "Damn it! Just let me help you."

Allan's desperation intrigued her. Without the shift of an eye, Laura leaned in to grace him with a kiss, which she assumed would end as suddenly as she had initiated it;

instead, Allan pulled her chin closer to him with a soft caress as she slowly lowered her hands to his waist.

The room contained a suffocating mist as the two became lost in the miracle of a magnetism too strong to break free. Sophie nudged the slightly opened door and interrupted them. Ashamed, they parted. Heads lowered, they refused to acknowledge that Sophie's presence had shattered the intense build-up of passion between them.

"I'm sorry," Sophie said, eyes lowered. She attempted a quick exit, but slowed a moment to explain. "I knew yah was upset, Ms. Laura, and I just wanted tuh check on yah, but I see yah just fine, ma'am." Sophie bowed her head gently and closed the door.

"I'm sorry. I can't do this. This is not my purpose." Laura retreated to the other end of the room.

"Don't be sorry. Sometimes while we're serving one purpose, we stumble on another," Allan pleaded.

"No, I can't believe—." Laura shook her head in disbelief of her actions.

Frustrated, Allan spoke, "You can believe what you want, and talk to me about what happened here later, but we should go, and soon. We can take a train tonight. All of us."

"I haven't fulfilled my cause here yet."

"And you won't with the UNIA against you. This isn't the only place that needs your message. We should reach farther."

"I will not fear, but I will accept the opportunity to spend time away from here where I'll be safe."

"Let me make arrangements to travel back to Jacksonville. Pack your things. I'll gather Sophie and the kids."

"In a few days," Laura said. Allan froze in place. "Please. The promises I've made to those who need guidance must be fulfilled."

"No. Tonight," he coldly insisted.

"I will not."

Allan stared at her boldly, but knew he was powerless against her insistent demeanor.

"I just ask that you pack your things. Can we at least agree to prepare to leave soon? We've been here long enough. Can you agree?" He concealed the monster that surfaced when he did not get his way.

"I will organize my belongings for a quick transition when the time comes."

"Thank you."

Once Allan left the room, Laura moved over to the dresser and pulled clothing from the drawer. She caught a glimpse of herself in the mirror above the dresser, and stared blankly, but could not determine what she saw there.

Sophie stood near the door to Allan's room, adjacent to hers, and drank water from a glass. He did not acknowledge her, but pushed open the door, stormed inside, and immediately gathered luggage from the closet.

"Where are the children?" he asked her through the open door.

Disturbed, Sophie twisted her body to respond, "They playin' in the room." She took a sip from the glass, walked into Allan's room, and placed it on a table with a loud *clack*.

"We have to pack. We're leaving as soon as I can reach some friends of mine and catch a train out of here."

Sophie spoke quietly, "You wanna have her fuh yah self, don't you? Gone steal a woman from her mission—the very thing that drives her? This won't end well, I know it."

Allan approached Sophie to offer clarity. "I've done nothing but respect that woman back there." He patted his chest. "I can't help how I feel for her." He backed away sensing he had moved too close.

"Kissin' ain't much for respect, 'specially wit' a woman like Ms. Laura," she whispered, "and God knows what else yah got up yah sleeve."

Allan opened the luggage on the bed and, disgusted, he said, "I never thought you saw anything but good in me." He walked over to the closet and removed a stack of folded clothes.

"You a man. I've seen my share, and I know how yah are. Poor Ms. Laura probably don't know what hit her."

Allan snickered. "Figures you would say that. Whatever just hit Ms. Laura back there, is not like what's been hitting you these past years. I would stay in my place if I were you," he said with finality.

Allan packed clothes into a suitcase as Sophie, at a loss for words, retreated to her bedroom.

~

The group lingered in Miami a while longer, and the following evening, the stage was set for Laura to speak to yet another crowd in UNIA-run Liberty Hall. She was nauseous. Her palms sweat and trembled, but Laura could not determine if what she felt was tension brought upon the event by the gossip that had been spread about her, or her own anxiety and frustration. Yet, she pressed on, and believed the plan of God was to show up despite the rift and underhanded table talks amongst a people she had once been eager to serve alongside.

Laura stood behind the podium before a crowd of nearly three hundred people when there was commotion at the back of the room. She did not open her mouth to speak, and would rather pretend she had not noticed. She had reason to be alarmed and cautious. Suddenly, two shots rang out; shattered glass crumbled to the floor as attendees screamed in fear. Immediately, the room grew dark.

Garveyites had succeeded in their plan to shoot out the lights in Liberty Hall, and it startled Laura into submission of Allan's suggestion. By sunrise the following morning, Laura, Sophie, Rachel, and Jessie arrived at Union Terminal in Jacksonville.

Once at Allan's home, Laura stepped out of the vehicle, inhaled deeply, and took in her surroundings. She noticed the stillness of the air, and the unexpected void of Allan's absence.

The two children ran ahead and pushed at a tire swing that dangled from a tree in the front yard—the work of the neighborhood kids who desired a space of their own to play, especially since most parks were off limits to people of their pigment.

The driver removed their suitcases and toted them to the stoop before he chugged off. Laura looked up the road each way, but nothing was there. She held tightly to the neck of her sweater.

As Sophie passed her, she said, "He ain't comin' this way for another week, Ms. Laura." Laura permitted Sophie to know. She allowed herself to be vulnerable, and did not deny that which Sophie was clearly aware.

Sophie's steps quickened as she made a beeline towards the overflowing mailbox. One letter at a time, she rummaged through the stack. Near the end, her disappointment was apparent. Sophie had not received the notification she awaited—acceptance into the Brewster nursing program.

That night, Laura sat quietly at the kitchen table while Sophie groomed her hair. Laura wrote a letter of her own— one she attempted to conceal as Sophie stood over her. It read:

*Dear Father, I miss you dearly. There is so much to share, but I have an urgent request…*

Sophie interrupted Laura's concentration. "Yah speakin' tomorrow. Nervous?"

Laura continued to write despite the distraction. "Very few people could ever know or understand what it feels like to take the platform, and to have no knowledge of what to say until the Lord gives it to you. I am always nervous; it keeps me humble and trusting."

"Yah just make it seem so easy," Sophie said as Laura continued to write. "Well, this won't be so easy fuh me to say."

"What's that Sophie?"

"My husband—." Sophie halted the comb in Laura's hair, dug into her roots to secure it, and took a seat next to her.

"What's the matter? Is he alright?"

"He's fine. Too fine, perhaps. Heard about some woman he got up north. Heard it from a ole friend. I try not tuh think much of it, but I know it don't mean nothin'." Sophie stood again and continued to comb Laura's hair. "He's coming fuh us. That's what I know."

"Coming for you? How? When—?"

"He had—uhh—sent a letter just sayin' he was comin'. Can't stop 'em from doin' what he feels. Right, Ms. Laura?"

"I don't believe that's what *he* feels."

Sophie shrugged, "Could be. Who's tuh say?"

"Your fear. How would he know you were here? And now, of all times. We spent weeks south of here. But now—with all that's transpired—and I saw you today. The mailbox. This other woman. You can't go back, Sophie. I know it looks impossible, but it all just takes time."

Sophie laughed softly. "No, Ms. Laura. It's none of those things. It's really what *he* wants. And I reckon it's what I want, too—at least to try."

Laura stood quickly, faced the woman, clasped both of her hands within her own, and pleaded with her. "What do *you* want? You're going to run away before the manifestation of what you've been asking for. And I know what's in your heart. Don't quit here."

"Well, I can't stop a man from coming fuh his wife." Sophie smiled with her lips, but her eyes were sad.

"And I guess I can't stop you from leaving with him." Laura realized she may have overstepped her position, and settled on the fact that she truly loved Sophie. She breathed deeply and released the tension of her full lips and tight forehead. "Forgive me if I've meddled in your personal affairs. I just know how much more you deserve."

"I know it. Yah mean well, Ms. Laura. But I believe he

means well too."

God had given Sophie freewill to make her own decisions regarding her marriage and the affairs of her family, but Laura believed she could see through the blinders Sophie so graciously wore. Although she was not confident of God's will for Sophie's life, and her relationship with such a violent man, she knew she could pray for peace, for Sophie's guidance, and for her to be able to see what could not be easily spoken.

# CHAPTER
# ELEVEN

As she had done prior to her involvement with the UNIA, Laura spoke here and there, and every subpar region that could use improvement, inspiration, or a fresh vision that would ease the frustration and lack that flowed as oil through black communities. There were moments when she contemplated her return to Africa, but with the morning sun, and renewed strength, she never settled on the completion of her assignment. Each moment she thought it best to leave for home fueled her desire to stay.

A week had passed since the group were run out of Miami because of Garvey's accusations of theft and deception. Although she had occasionally heard the statements being made against her, Laura refused to give life to what she considered already dead.

A church on the edge of Jacksonville burst at its seams, and caused a few to stand outside closest to the windows to be in earshot of Laura's powerful message. Many listeners found themselves anew—no longer did they doubt their ability, nor God's authority. They thirsted, and she poured out all that was within her; they drank and were filled. Laura, overcome with passion, shouted her words across the pews.

"Don't see me," she corrected, "see the Christ-spirit that works in and through me to you. If God leaves me, I am nothing. He only uses me as an instrument. It is He that speaks through me to you. It is not my will that I am here, but God's. It is not for me that I am here, but for you. When my journey is over, I will rest in the arms of my Father. I have given my life for His work, sometimes unwillingly, but His grace has propelled me to do more, to desire more for His people."

The sea of black faces glistened and empowered Laura to pour out her Master's love for a people who had been lost, trampled upon and burdened. Her heart required grace to carry it, and she wept. Laura made her best attempt to convince such a people that God had not abandoned them, and that His plan was greater than the hardships they faced. They had been born into a body that was beautifully crafted by the Creator of all things, yet were despicable to those who seemed to have earthly power.

Overwhelmed by the magnitude of God presence, she took a second to gather herself, and wiped her face with a small towel. When her vision cleared, she noticed the crowd shift. A familiar, towering figure lingered at the rear of the room. It was Allan. An ocean of thoughts flooded her mind in an instant, and none of them aligned with the message she delivered that evening. She stumbled over words in her attempt to reposition her thoughts.

"To—to desire more for His people." She swallowed as much saliva as she could gather, and the crowd stared in wait of her next statement. "What will you sacrifice today? Sacrifice. Few care to hear the word. To give up, to let go, to no longer desire, and then to not regret. We steer clear of sacrifice, but it is sacrifice that pushes us to our destiny. Jesus' sacrifice was greater than any that God expects from any of us. His sacrificial death was so that we would live.

Are you living?" She took a sip of water from a tin mug Sophie handed her.

"For many of you, your goal is to survive—or some of you have settled, and become satisfied with that. Glory to glory! Prosperity! Mere survival is beneath the means of God. He is your source of strength, and your sacrifice will not be in vain. What are you willing to give up, and what work has God willed you to do? When you've made peace with both, you will walk in full purpose, and in the glory of Almighty God."

A roar went up all over the sanctuary. Those who stood beyond its walls whistled and shouted as loud as the crowd who celebrated within them. While some made a beeline for the door to escape into the cool, fall air, others desired to connect further with Laura. They approached with a heart that yearned to be confirmed, or a mind that sought understanding and clarity, or with hands eager to do the work she so eloquently described as possible for the progress of their people.

She greeted the attendees, offered hugs to men and women, and kissed the young. She breathed words of life and encouragement, and spoke directly to the situations each visitor had consistently taken to God in their private prayers. Laura was confident and bold, and those who encountered her left her presence completely comforted.

"It's an honor, ma'am," a male parishioner approached and shook Laura's hand. "Please, tell me what I can do. I don't have much, but I'm able-bodied, and I have two boys too. One twelve and the other thirteen."

"There is much to be done," Laura responded, "and I dare not turn away anyone with a heart such as yours." She smiled.

"I'm Otis. I live about eight blocks west of here on Duncan Street. The only one by that name, so if you inquire around, you're sure to find me, ma'am."

"I will not forget it." Sophie stood near Laura with a writing pad and quickly scribbled the information. Laura smiled as she dotingly pat Otis on the back.

Several expressed their gratitude for her presence in Jacksonville, and others requested a word of prayer. Nearly an hour passed since the conclusion of her message, but she was not yet weary, even after the crowd dwindled down to a single woman. Allan waited patiently until Laura greeted the woman before he finally approached.

He smirked, "It didn't take long to get back to it up here, I see."

"There is something about this place. They are thirsting for change." She beamed.

The two saw that they were alone, aside from a woman who swept the floor, so they began a slow traipse towards the church's exit.

"And you're the one to help bring it about? This change you mentioned?" Allan asked.

Laura said, humbly, "Thank you."

"For what?"

"For knowing when to move. I can be stubborn, I know, but I can see more clearly here. The barges, the river, all great access for trade. The people, all in need of a word from God."

"It sounds like you'll have your work cut out for you."

"This is only the beginning."

When they made their way to the rear, the two exited the building as Allan held the door open. Two police cars sat quietly near the short driveway of the church, and a crowd of people stood far off to witness what was happening without getting involved.

Laura inquisitively approached one of the cars where an officer stood, but Allan grabbed her arm to hold her back.

"Wait a minute," he told her, and tugged at her arm. "Don't approach them."

The officer stood as tall as his spine would allow, tilted his head back slightly in case it was not enough, and sneered at the two of them.

"What's going on here?" Allan asked the officer.

"We have cause to believe that Laura Kofi—that is you, right?" Laura nodded. "She's been accused of fraud, and it's also said that she is a root worker. You know, that voodoo carrying on." He laughed at the idea and pulled an envelope into plain slight. "This warrant for her arrest is for fraud."

Laura looked devastated as her eyes darted the crowd. Two shadows, seemingly satisfied, walked away from the scene and into the darkness.

"We need to take her in for questioning," the officer continued to address Allan.

Laura turned her attention back to the officers. "Who said such a thing against me?" she asked.

"I am not at liberty to say. Turn around." He reached into his back pocket and withdrew a pair of handcuffs as he maneuvered Laura around with his other hand.

"You don't have to handcuff her. She's done nothing wrong," Allan insisted. The officer proceeded to handcuff her, and ignored Allan's plea.

"It is only fair that I know my accuser," Laura said as she complied with the officer's commands. The officer twisted Laura's shoulder.

"God dammit!" Allan lashed out. "I said she won't cause you trouble."

Laura extended her free hand in front of Allan while the officer firmly gripped the other behind her back. "Peace. All is well. I'm fine, Allan."

Laura allowed the officer to cuff both hands; she shrieked as his forcefulness caused discomfort, and then ducked into the back of his car before she was driven away.

After leaving the children in the care of a parishioner who lived next to the church—an attempt to keep them out of harm's way—Sophie joined Allan. They watched the two vehicles continue up the road and completely out of sight.

The jail was nestled near the quietly flowing river only a ten-minute trip from where Laura was picked up. She sat quietly, and reasoned within herself the tactic of the enemy to see her give up, turn away, and return to Africa. It could not be the God who had called her to sacrifice for His kingdom. *Right?* She refused to give in, and settled in her heart to face whatever would come.

When she arrived, Laura was immediately photographed, and then escorted into a separate room where she was made to strip down to her underwear. She had never openly exposed herself to one of the opposite gender, and especially those whose skin were as white as salt. She attempted to conceal herself, so covered her womanly parts with each of her hands. The officers from the scene of her arrest watched in suppressed excitement.

"You have been accused of fraud and of carrying voodoo roots on your person, girl. I'll need to search you," he said. He did not ask permission, but made his intent to touch her clear.

"But I wear barely anything now. You can see there is nothing here." The officer approached without regard for her plea. "I beg you, sir," Laura said desperately. Her lips trembled as she contemplated what more to say.

Abrasive, the officer yelled, "Turn around!" He pushed Laura's bare shoulder and forced her to comply with his command. "Lift your arms, girl."

Laura slowly lifted her arms, and the officer removed her bra. He stood behind her as her full, round breasts rested gently on her chest and casted a perfect feminine silhouette on the wall in front of her. He grabbed her chest, salivated, but concealed his pleasure.

"Under garments," he demanded as he backed a foot away.

A single tear cascaded down Laura's cheek as she bent over to remove her panties. The officer watched intently, and then walked around to gaze at her completely nude frontal.

"Open your legs," he barked.

Laura gasped and attempted to restrain herself. She did as she was told. The officer stooped to look between her thighs, and then stood again.

"Get dressed," he snarled.

Both officers left the room, and Laura released a wail of humiliation—one laced with brokenness and sorrow.

~

That night, while abandoned in the darkness of a cage, Laura dreamed—a dream that mirrored the events which led her to that very moment. In it, the African jungle illuminated the background of an airy room where Princess Laura rested in bed. White cloth draped over her forehead and beads of sweat gathered on her chest. Two nurses from the village were at her aid. Laura sat quickly and vomited violently before she laid back again. She murmured, but her words were impossible to make out.

"This fever is quite severe," one of the nurses said. "We'll need to alarm the king." The other nurse agreed, and they left Laura alone in the room.

She turned onto her side in agony and prayed. "Lord, please. I have disobeyed You. Make me well, and I will do what You say." She quivered for a moment before she closed her eyes. Soon, she was completely still and totally at rest.

When Laura awoke in jail the following day, back in the reality of her arrest, she heard the rattle of keys. She stood and wiped the sleep from her eyes to see clearly. An officer opened the jail cell and, without sufficient evidence of her alleged crimes, released Laura to go home.

She emerged from the jail a free woman, but something was arrested within her that would never be free again. She felt like a bullseye, a target whose paint could not be altered—one whose apologies would never make room or lend favor. She was black. Intelligent, but black. Anointed, but black. Gifted, but black. And to those who lacked pigment like her own, her intentions, or the light with which she was seen, was as dark as her complexion. To them, she was nothing greater, and for a moment, she believed it too.

Sophie ran up to Laura and embraced her tightly after she emerged from the jail, but Laura first noticed Allan, who hopelessly stood off in the distance.

"How yah feelin', Ms. Laura? I cooked yah somethin' good at home," Sophie pressed the loose coils on Laura's head back into place and tried to make light of the circumstances. "I know yah just as anxious to get there as we are tuh have yah back. Even a single night is too long without yah." Sophie smiled faintly.

Laura heard Sophie clearly, but her attention rested on Allan. It was not long before Sophie noticed that her words were without reach, and looked to what had captured Laura's attention. "He almost lost his mind there without yah. Never seen a man work so hard tuh get the truth and make it right." She paused a moment, and then she whispered, "He means well, Ms. Laura."

Laura walked over to Allan and, with solemn eyes, he examined her. For a while they said nothing, but their silence unified them—passion moved like fire on a wave of unspoken understanding. He opened the car door for her and she stepped forth.

Close enough to employ a whisper, Allan asked, "Did they hurt you?"

"Not my body." She lowered her head and took a seat in the vehicle. "I'm still re-assembling the fragments of my pride." The process would take longer than Laura could imagine it would—and would not come as quickly as the commute home.

# CHAPTER
# TWELVE

The Florida air was damp, hot, and carried mosquitoes lazily through its dense haze as Laura guided several men over a plot of bare land. The men swatted and frequently wiped the sweat from their foreheads with handkerchiefs or the backside of their hands to remain attentive to the cause which Laura had lured them out to hear.

Laura pointed, "We'll build the sanctuary here. And around the building—a few homes and a community store." She paused as she recognized the look of impossibility smeared across the faces of her listeners—men who were frequently present and committed to the vision of her ministry. "Materials will be here as soon as next week. And I'm sure you men will do exactly what must be done." She smiled and announced, "This will be the African Universal Church."

A man spoke from the small crowd of helpers, "Yes, Mother." He returned a smile before he departed with the rest of the group.

Allan stayed behind as the others disappeared into the

distance.

"Mother? Where did that come from?" he asked.

"I can't say. One day I looked up and it was 'Mother Kofi' this, and 'Mother Kofi' that. It is a term of endearment, and respect. I am well honored," she said as she stared at the bare land.

Allan kicked a few pebbles resting near his feet. "Well, you don't seem like one who'd want them—children, I mean—anytime soon."

"Not a lot of thought. I think they are blessings, but I want to be ready for the weight of motherhood. The village is always great, but the core must first be strong."

"You seem mighty strong to me, little lady."

"I can only try." She shrugged.

Each morning, Laura raced the rooster's crow to the building site; she would dig, and pile, and push. Sweat beaded above her brows, but she never wiped it away. Laura merely turned her head towards the east and allowed the wind to grace her forehead with a cool breeze.

Labor was consistent and plenty—men and women who loved Laura, her ministry, and her vision, gathered as often as possible—before work, after school—to help however they could. Over 50 people would work from sun up until dusk. Laura insisted they go home at a decent hour, but they were determined to finish, and with haste. Sophie ensured everyone was well fed, and prepared sandwiches or a hearty stew and rice for them to fill their bellies.

It was near quitting time when the sun's light gave way to darkness, and the small lanterns they carried to light their paths home were not enough to illuminate the work site. One by one, they grabbed their belongings, some children, said their farewells, and started home.

"Ms. Laura," Allan approached, shirt drenched in sweat.

Laura, who painted eagerly in the dim light, was so determined to complete her task before she lost the sun, she did not hear him. Each brush stroke brought a major victory as the seconds shoved away at the sun. Without a response,

Allan walked closer to the fixated woman. Before he reached down to claim her attention, Allan's shadow was cast over the white paint and immediately startled Laura, and caused her to lose her balance.

"Ms. Laura. It's Allan," he said as he reached out for her. "You afraid?"

Face pressed firmly against the freshly painted wall, she reached out for Allan's hand. White paint was smeared across nearly half of her chestnut skin. Allan attempted to contain his laughter, and failed.

"It's not funny," she said. She wiped the dirt from her navy-blue skirt, which nearly dusted the ground.

"I'm sorry, Ms. Laura, but I'd beg to differ." Allan released the buildup of his laughter; and before long, Laura chuckled a bit as well. "You're really looking the African part today. Now you have the paint to go with that accent."

"Ha, ha. You're to blame," Laura said, and gathered her pail of paint and a tray of brushes. "Sneaking up behind me. You ought to be ashamed." She shuffled off.

"Ms. Laura, don't be that way," he chuckled as he walked after her. "I didn't mean to laugh." He tried to resist. "See, I'm serious now." He pressed his lips together as though they were glued, but could not keep them still enough to convince her.

Laura carried a load of supplies in one hand, and clenched her garment with the other to get away swiftly. She ignored Allan's call, and continued to walk—an action void of any sincerity. She quickened her pace, and Allan cheerfully jogged after her. Laura's heart was light.

The two of them laughed in the moonlit night, and then slowed and watched as Jessie approached from a short distance. The boy seemed to be in a hurry, and staggered a bit before he quickly caught his footing.

"Hey, Jessie!" Allan called out as the boy shuffled near. "Tell Ms. Laura here to lighten up a little." He chuckled without constraint. "This here is a history lesson, boy. Our people. Welcome to Africa!"

Laura turned and nudged Allan's shoulder as she burst into laughter. "Not fair," she giggled.

"I'm just saying, if we don't get this up and running, *this* might be the closest he'll come to it."

"I would have you know, there are people over there who do not wear tribal paint," she retorted.

"Well, let me——." Allan's playfulness was interrupted by the boy when he pressed his small palm against Allan's sweat-drenched shirt. "What is it?"

Jessie handed a note, folded rigidly, over to Allan and then buried his face into Laura's dense skirt.

Allan read silently, but his body hinted at its contents. His eyes strained to read the writing as the light had been completely lost. For a moment, his shoulder slumped over. He took repetitive, shallow breaths. Laura grew more curious by the caresses of the evening wind about the news he received. Allan realized he had an audience, so folded the note and placed it in his pocket. He lifted his head and opened his eyes wide to allow the breeze to irritate them into dryness.

"What is it?" Laura asked.

"It's my aunt—up north." He paused, and then looked to the boy. "Come on, Jessie. Let's get you home and ready for learning tomorrow." He lightly gripped the boy's shoulder, which maneuvered him to march in front of them. He leaned in closer to Laura as they walked, and spoke as privately as he could in the presence of a third pair of ears. "Grandma. She's gone."

Laura immediately felt the weight of Allan's loss of someone so treasured, and wanted to hug him. She dropped the pail and brush to the ground, and quickly embraced Allan as tightly as each muscle would permit. The sweat of his shirt permeated hers.

"I'm sorry," Laura whispered closely into his ear.

Allan said nothing, but finessed himself out of her embrace—a silent request to keep some distance—and the three of them walked on without another word.

Allan's silence continued through the next afternoon when he finally gained enough of an appetite to enter the dining area and take a seat at the table. Sophie poured boiling grits from pot to bowl, and then placed a pan of fried fish in the center. Already seated there, Laura followed each of Allan's steps, and desired to reverse the grief plastered over his countenance. Sophie slowed her pace to honor the time of mourning for the man who had entered.

"Heah," Sophie said softly as she placed a glass of water on the table in front of Allan. He slid it closer, but did not lift it to take a drink. He hung his head, and the entire atmosphere became gray and lifeless.

"It pleases me that you are here to eat. It could do some good," Laura said.

"Is there somethin' different I can get yah?" Sophie asked as she joined them at the table.

"No—no. This will do just fine." He reached for a piece of fish.

"I know you'll be travelling for the burial," Laura said. She stirred her bowl of grits. "And it may be good to not go alone." Allan perked up a moment and looked at Laura. "Maybe I can come with you."

"No. I can manage."

"That was not being questioned. You don't have to go alone. Please, allow me."

Overcome by all he felt, Allan stood quickly, shielded his face from the women's observation, and left the room.

~

People gathered outside the house built of parallel wooden planks. It jutted slightly out of a hill and created the two-story dwelling that held in its shadow a small burial plot. Some visitors whispered amongst themselves, others laughed on occasion. Reflections of the little woman they called "Liza", or "Ma Liza" if you were of relation, could be heard from the front to the back of the house. Young ones somberly watched the grave as though it would move, certain they would be quick enough to catch it.

Although exhausted from his travels, Allan arrived upbeat, and mustered as much energy as the pain of loss would allow. He had not spoken much to Laura in the time since they departed Jacksonville, and she assumed his grief was in full force, which naturally would hinder any outward expression. Laura followed him quietly after she sensed his ego desired to secretly mourn the loss of his grandmother.

Two teenage girls were perched on the porch's railing. One of them noticed Allan as he approached the steps leading to the front door. She tapped the other girl—who gazed into the distance—on the shoulder. "Look!"

"Al!" they yelled excitedly as they ran toward him.

He locked them both in an embrace and said, "Girls, it's good to see you."

They withdrew their grip as if they remembered their mournful purpose for the reunion, and somberly looked at each other. A few visitors had become aware of the arrival of a new guest, so as Laura looked about, she nodded and slightly waved to those whose attention she had captured.

"Girls, this is Ms. Laura. A good friend." They both took a turn and hugged her. "These are my little cousins."

While the interaction transpired, something caught Allan's attention a few yards away—more specifically, someone. Someone Allan had not seen since he was a boy. To be sure of himself, Allan blinked his eyes and squinted as he looked. The man stood near an old rocking chair, and stared dotingly as it swayed slightly by the force of the wind. The collar of his coat was stiff around his ears and occasionally brushed against his poorly groomed beard. The man lifted his hands from his pocket and rubbed them together as though they were cold before he finally noticed his observer. The man was Allan's father, Richard.

"My mama's inside," one of the girls said.

"Yeah, cooking away," the other contributed. "She don't

want help, but we tried." The girl shrugged.

Allan broke his focus, wrapped his arms around both girls, and together they traipsed past his father to enter the house. Richard gawked with empty eyes as they went.

"Al! Is that you?" A woman, who placed a dish on the short, round kitchen table, approached quickly and extended herself for a hug.

"Aunt June, I sure missed you."

"We all missed you here too—especially Ma Liza." They released each other from their embrace and Allan hung his head as he removed his hat. "Now, don't you go feeling a thing about it. She was uh old lady. You know that."

"I just got so busy running around. I could have come to see her."

"For what?" June pressed her small hand against Allan's shoulder. "Using what she put in you, helping people, was more important than sitting around here these last few years. Her mind was about gone." June walked away and shifted a few dishes on the table. "Go in there and get those beans from the stove for me."

Allan turned and exposed Laura's presence. "Who's this?" June inquired.

"Al's friend, Ms. Laura," one of the girls offered.

June extended her hand and it was met by Laura's. "Nice to meet you."

"I am greatly sorry for your loss."

"Your voice—the accent. Where you from?" June asked as she moved back towards the table.

"Accra—the Gold Coast of Africa."

"That's nowhere near here." June stirred a pot of rice. "How do you know Al?"

"Our work together. He has been so gracious and kind to accompany and guide me."

Allan returned with the hot pot of beans, which he carried with a damp kitchen towel, and placed it on the table. "I'm sorry I didn't introduce you two." He wiped his moist hands on his coat before taking it off. "Where's grandma?"

he asked.

"The great room," June whispered as she turned away and continued to busy herself with the meal.

Several guests stood near a wooden casket draped with pale yellow fabric and adorned with flowers the youngsters collected from around the community. Inside rested a woman whose wrinkles folded heavily near her eyes and became the dominant feature of her face. Worn and ragged, she slept peacefully with her arms laid gently at her side. Allan clinched his hat between both hands as he approached her. After he gazed affectionately at the woman who had raised him from birth, he gently brushed her hair with the back of his hand. The touch of her lifeless body pushed a button and released every speck of emotion he had contained; he sobbed without restraint. His wails sent a wave of sorrow through the room, and those who stood near began to weep.

"It's okay," a deep, male voice spoke from behind Allan as a hand rested on his shoulder. After a moment, Allan gathered himself enough to notice the source of the voice. He stood tall, wiped his face with his hands, and lifted his chin.

"It's alright now. She was around a mighty long time. No need in getting everybody all worked up," Richard spoke, and rested his hand on Allan's back to reinforce his words.

"Uncle Richard?" Allan flicked his hand away. "You should only speak when you've been spoken to, and I don't recall parting my lips to say a damn thing to you."

Aunt June entered the room where mourners stood quietly to witness the altercation between the two men who stood close enough to embrace but was prevented by deep, unseen tension. "What's going on in here?" she asked.

"Nothing," Allan responded. "Uncle Richard was just leaving me the hell alone, and sitting his old ass down somewhere." Allan's father backed away.

"That's disrespectful, Al, and you know it. Ma

wouldn't have ever allowed you to—."

Allan looked at June with disgust. "Don't you tell me what Ma would have done," he said forcefully. "I know what she did. She took me in when this bastard here ran away."

"She protected the both of you, Allan. You wouldn't understand unless you lived through what they lived through, or saw all the disgusting things Ma Liza saw done to other niggers."

"How would he know what would happen, Aunt June? He didn't stick around long enough to see."

"Black men, white girls—black men die for way less than that. You should know—."

"And I wasn't worth the risk? I mean—all these years? He could've come back when I was two or so when all the curiosity had died down, but he didn't. This coward kept running like someone was after him."

"No need to defend me, June," Richard spoke. "I came to pay respects to Ma—not to deal with this ungrateful bastard."

"Ungrateful?" Allan retorted. "For *you*? What have you ever done for me?"

"I left you in good hands you son of a bitch," he yelled and lashed towards Allan before he was stopped by June, who held him back with all her might. "There wasn't anyone more capable of making you the man you are than that woman laying right there. That was my mama." Richard backed away from June and sobbed. "I didn't want to do it. She'd caught wind of the suspicions, and she sent me away. I didn't want to go. I slept in ditches some nights when I had nowhere else to lay my head. I couldn't come home. I wanted my warm bed back, my old life back; but more than that, I wanted Ma. And you had her. I wasn't a man yet, but it was her who told me to keep my distance. My God, I didn't want to—but she loved me enough to carry the weight I would die carrying. And *she* did it." He gestured towards Allan. "Look at you. She taught us all to read, but you've done something with your learning. You travel all over. You don't think I want to say I had something to do with that? But I credit her. I won't ever take it from her. Today, I want to honor her. If you don't give a damn about much else, respect that."

Richard walked out and the screen door slammed shut behind him. Everyone in the room stared at Allan, curious of his next move. He merely kneeled next to his grandmother and shared a final moment in the presence of her physical form.

Near sundown, as the sky was painted with peaches and plums, when all the eating had been done, and after Laura helped to put the dishes away, she joined Allan on the porch. He sat in his grandmother's favorite rocking chair, one she had used to soothe crying babies, to relax from her daily duties, or to teach the children she would gather around her.

"Can I get you anything?" Laura offered.

"No, I'm fine," he said coldly.

She wrestled with what to say next. "I'll take the next train back in the morning if it's alright with you."

"I told you I didn't need you to come in the first place. I don't even know why you're here."

"Because it's what I choose. It's not for you to tell others how they should care for you."

He stood and looked at her sharply. "Don't think you know a damn thing about me because you had a front row seat to that debacle between me and Richard. You know nothing."

"I may not know much about that, but I know your pain runs deep. You are looking for—."

"Dammit!" Allan desired to leave, but was compelled to finally dump out his frustrations. "I hope you didn't come along to minister to me. It's not going to work. I don't need another lesson." He walked towards the entry of the house. Laura parted her lips to speak, but nothing would come out. "You can stay on the couch. I'll have the girls get you whatever you need, and in the morning, I'll have someone take you back to the station." He walked into the house, and Laura stood alone near the creaking chair.

The house was quiet aside from the tick of the clock upon the mantle. Laura slept little. Through the night, she passed the time in reflection. She rested on the fact that there was nothing to be done about Allan's circumstance—that only God could alter his perception of those who loved him, or soften his willingness to truly understand. She no longer wrestled against his ego, but maintained her care and concern for him.

In the moments before dawn, as the crickets began their slumber, Laura heard something shuffle around outside. Initially, she dismissed the noise. Perhaps an animal had wandered onto the property. The sound lingered. It was footsteps crunching against the gravel. Laura sat up on the couch and peeked out the window. Initially, she saw nothing. Her eyes darted the lawn; and there it was. The figure of a woman dressed in a dark-colored skirt, a coat, and a wide-brim hat stood over the fresh earth recently piled on top of Ma Liza. The woman did not move, and seemed to silently salute the buried woman. Laura watched, and believed it was one of Ma Liza's granddaughters who had come back to pay another visit to the dead.

As the sun began to *shoo* the darkness, Laura kept watch. The woman must have sensed she had drawn the attention of a stranger. She turned quickly, and noticed Laura, who stared from behind the curtain. A bolt of electricity flowed from Laura's fingertips to her toes in an instant. The woman she observed had skin as pale as milk—her face was haggard and troubled. Laura moved away from the curtains, and laid down for what seemed like mere seconds. And when she sat up to look from the window again, the woman was no longer there.

# CHAPTER THIRTEEN

Laura took an early train back to Jacksonville the morning after Allan's grandmother had been delicately laid to rest, and left him behind to sort things out with relatives. There, he would have the space he so desperately needed from Laura. The burden of her travels may have made Laura weary in mind and body, but she left behind any emotional remnants of Allan's remarks.

When she entered the home she shared with Sophie, Allan, and the children, Laura nearly stumbled over two large suitcases that waited at the door. One belonged to Sophie, and the other to Rachel. She shoved them aside, and scanned the room for the owners, but the room was still and cold. There were no giggles, or children chasing one another, no one coming in or going out, no aroma of baked pie or fried chicken in the air.

"Sophie. Rachel," she called, and immediately Sophie emerged. She beamed with a gigantic smile, and took Laura's travel bag from her hand.

"I'm glad yuh back heah safe, Ms. Laura." Sophie gently

nudged Laura in the direction of her bedroom. "I know yah tired."

"I am. Where are you off to?" She gestured towards the door. "These are your belongings by the entry?"

"Don't mind yahself wit' that, Ms. Laura." Sophie smiled nervously and continued to escort Laura to the back of the home.

"Are you leaving, Sophie?" Laura paused and attempted to lock eyes with the woman, but Sophie resisted.

"Just for a lil' while, ma'am. He's comin' t'night, and we off tuh make things work."

Laura examined Sophie's countenance—determined and completely set on what she had already prepared for. Laura seemed to rope Allan's comments from the previous evening into her thoughts; it worked its way down to her throat and choked her. Laura found it hard to swallow; and although she wanted to pour out all she felt about Sophie's decision to leave, she bottled it up instead and did not speak. She gently grabbed her bag from Sophie's hand, opened it up, and removed three folded bills. Laura stuffed them into Sophie's hands as she clenched them tightly.

"I can't take this, Ms. Laura. Yah already gave me pay this week and plenty else," Sophie said.

"It's not pay. It's a gift. Use it when you need it, or save it if you don't. God has you covered no matter where you go." In an instant, Laura drew in the weight of the moment—the parting of a dear friend—and the rope tightened. "Thank you," she said. Her lips trembled as she tucked her bag beneath her arm, lifted her chin, and walked away from the woman who so desperately wanted to leave. And in that manner, Laura accepted the disbandment of her tribe.

Sophie placed the folded money between the crease of her breasts, recently spritzed with perfume, when there was a firm knock on the door.

"A minute please," Sophie called sweetly, and fixed her dress. She quickly ran her fingers along the edges of her hair, which was pulled up into a full, tight bun.

She nudged the front door, and it creaked open. Jack stood there, clad in a clean, collared shirt and dark slacks. His beard was freshly trimmed; his eyes were bright with optimism but tinged with secrecy. He was quietly poised, and the shadow of his presence escaped him and was cast immediately over the petite Sophie.

"Jack," Sophie exhaled and examined him. "You look good." He handed her a small arrangement of flowers, pulled her closely and then kissed her cheek. His nose rested on her forehead, and a sense of the familiar comforted the two.

"I missed you," he whispered. She felt the warmth of his breath against her skin. "Come with me."

"I will," she said playfully, and was released from his grip. "I have tuh get Rachel first. She's in the back."

"Hurry now. There's a train leaving for home in about an hour. We can't miss it." He pulled her closely again. "I can't wait for things to be like they used to."

Sophie remembered. "Hopefully not everything will be the same. Right?" she asked cautiously as she locked eyes with him.

"You know what I mean," he grinned. "Get her. Let's go."

"Rachel!" Sophie called. "Come up heah and see yah daddy." Sophie gathered the suitcases and handed them over to Jack. "Rachel!" she called again. She put on her sweater and realized her daughter had yet to respond. "Let me get her," she said to Jack before she walked away.

Soon, Sophie resurfaced with the young girl, and when she noticed her father, she grabbed her mother's leg and held tightly. "Rachel, come on. It's not time to play." Sophie attempted to loosen her grip, but it strengthened, and Rachel refused to release her. "Come on heah."

A squeal rang out; Rachel began to cry. Jack dropped the suitcases and gently approached. He kneeled next to her. "It's time to go now. Stop this foolishness."

Rachel stiffened—coiled around her mother's leg. "My lord, chile. What's the problem?" Sophie asked.

The Jack who entered the home stepped out of the moment, and a more recognizable creature stepped in. "She's being a brat. Must be somethin' you taught her in all this time you been away." His shift in tone caused Sophie to shudder, but her newfound strength forced her to resist the urge to surrender.

"I did no such thing. She ain't never like this," she said resentfully.

"Come on here, gal," Jack forcefully broke the bond between them, and Rachel cried loudly.

"Alright. That's enough. Let her 'lone." Sophie reached out for Rachel, but Jack lifted the crying girl into the air firmly by her waist. "Givva' tuh me, Jack."

"No, she alright. Now, let's go."

"No, Jack. Givva' tuh me now." Sophie had lived this moment before.

"She's spoiled, and I'll break her tail good when we get home."

"Give me her, Jack," Sophie said desperately.

"Don't you ever fix your mouth to give me demands, woman. This here belongs to me too," he said as he shook Rachel who squirmed in his arm.

"We ain't goin' nowhere. Put her down."

"You ain't?" He clenched his fist and his jaw simultaneously. "Get your shit and let's go."

"Yeah, I said it. I—we ain't goin' nowhere, Jack. Now, put her down and get outta heah!"

"Wait. What's this?" He examined Sophie as Rachel continued to struggle. He smirked, "You got another man, don't you?"

"What?" Sophie paused. "Please give me her," she said, and refused to entertain a speck of Jack's insecurities.

"It's all over you, Sophie. Dammit! Had me waste my time and money coming down here for y'alls worthless asses and you screwing around with someone else. He can have your ass, but he can't have her. She stays with me."

"Please, Jack. No!" Sophie screamed as she tried to rip Rachel from his arm.

"Bitch!" Jack swiftly thrusted out his hand. When it collided Sophie's face, like the sting of a hundred needles, she fell to the floor. "Go to hell."

Jack turned to leave with the dangling damsel whose sobs grew louder after she witnessed her mother's attack. With a false sense of victory resting on his broad shoulders, Jack was met face-to-steel with a shotgun before he could reach the door. Laura cocked it back.

"Put her down," she said firmly, and then looked over to Sophie who was unable to stop the blood that oozed from her nose.

"Don't be stupid, woman. Move."

"Stupid is choosing to know what it is like to be without a head."

"You wouldn't be so bold without that gun now, would you?"

"You'd reach the grave before you have the chance to know."

"Put it down now, bitch!" he growled, and then waited to see if Laura would lower the gun by his demand. She did not, and maintained focus on her target instead. "Here," he said, and placed Rachel on the ground. The girl immediately ran over to her mother who embraced her tightly.

Laura backed Jack out of the living room, hands slightly raised in surrender, as the barrel moved within inches of his nose.

"Don't come back here." Laura's finger rested firmly on the trigger; a hiccup could have discharged the shot.

"I'm leaving. I'm leaving," Jack complied. He looked at the women, bold and weak, and then walked away.

Laura closed and locked the door behind him without a sigh of hesitation, and then rested the shotgun in the corner. Stunned, Sophie was without words—or the pain of her throbbing nose was too intense to speak. She mustered a mere *thank you* as she caught some of the blood with her blouse, and revealed her bloodstained bra.

"Be prayerful of your every move," Laura said. "Sometimes life depends on it." Sophie swallowed every ounce of humble tea, and fully accepted Laura's shared wisdom as she poured.

~

Weeks passed, one after the other, and Laura had heard little from Allan. Extremely impersonal, he called one afternoon to check on the house—to see if any maintenance was necessary and to ensure the women and children were comfortable. It was then that Laura learned he had returned to Miami to assist with the work down there. It was needed more than ever since Garvey had been deported back to Jamaica in the days that surrounded Ma Liza's funeral.

Despite Garvey's absence, Laura continued to receive telephone threats and offensive letters that demanded she return to Africa. Numerous Garvey followers who resided in Jacksonville would show up to Laura's speaking engagements and protest openly. It was a reminder of his reach. If that was not enough, the February release of *Negro World* denounced Laura as a fake. Even with a sea between them, Garvey insisted "this woman is a fake and has no authority from me to speak to the United Negro Improvement Association."

Embarrassed and broken, Laura continued to minister in churches, speak in rallies, and host community workshops throughout the south. The UNIA's attempt to destroy her failed to hinder her movements under the authority and call of Christ.

~

The fumes of the freshly coated walls in the sanctuary were still in the air as congregants and visitors from various places made their way down the road. A tiny fingerprint could have permanently left its mark on the barely dried surface of the walls, but Laura was excited to begin the celebration, a service for the completion of the initial phase of African Universal Church.

The engagement drew a crowd of people from across the city—those who had heard her messages before. There was barely room for everyone to be seated, but despite what appeared to be success, Laura consistently scanned the room for a friend whose presence was not felt—Allan. Time did not mend or erase Laura's desire to make things right with him. She acknowledged the rift between them as something beyond her power to change, and she found strength in focus. So, as she had frequently done in his absence, Laura prepared herself to speak every word that mounted in her heart.

"Mother knows how St. Paul felt, and how all the Apostles felt when they were put in jail for His name's sake," she spoke from a small, wooden pulpit. "My God told me if I go back to Africa it is death, and if I stay here it is death, but if I die in His program over here, then I can be in His Spirit and be able to take care of Africa's children everywhere. If God deem me worthy to suffer and die in His Program for His people, then I tell Him, *thank you*. No man taketh my life. I give up my life that I might take it up again. All I've asked my Old Man God is to take me in the presence of my children that they may be witness that I went down for them.[1]"

---

[1] Weisenfeld, Judith, and Richard Newman. *This Far by Faith: Readings in African-American Womens Religious Biography*. Routledge, 1996.

# CHAPTER
# FOURTEEN

The Florida winter called for overcoats and scarves; but with spring on the horizon, the promise of warmer days and blossoming flowers meant, in time, Laura would again experience conditions like those of Accra—her native land. Mild weather would mean frequent travel and opportunities to reach those in open air events and rallies without the burden of chill. While it was a joy for Laura to connect with people indoors, she was accustomed to treks through warm climates where she soaked up the energy of the sun on her deep mocha skin. The cold conditions that surrounded her were unfavorable, but she maintained her glow, and her own flame had not been quenched.

"You can't come this time. There is more than enough that I must be mindful of, and there are plenty of hands here to keep up with you," Laura spoke softly to Jessie who sulked relentlessly on his bed. He shook his head in refusal and folded his arms tightly across his chest.

"But school is your duty and obligation. You cannot miss a full week." Laura stood, and believed she had asserted herself enough to be understood.

Stubbornly, Jessie walked over to the closet, pulled out a bag, and began to pack his things; he shoved in a pair of dark pants and a few collared shirts. Laura watched his quiet protest until Sophie walked by and took notice of the little boy who frantically pulled socks from a chest and packed them away.

"What's goin' on in heah?" Sophie inquired.

"Jessie would like to come back to Miami with us this week. But—," Laura turned to Jessie, "there are four engagements I must attend within the week, and possibly others. It's more than I would like to have him along for."

"Oh no, Jessie." Sophie said sympathetically, an attempt to comfort him. "You should stay put. Besides, Rachel will be heah, and those new friends you got will be round too. You'll be by yah'self on the road wit' us old folks."

Jessie continued to pack, and disregarded Sophie's remarks.

Laura was hopeless. "I guess it won't hurt for you to ride along." She paused. "But just this time. Your studies are more important."

Jessie's desperate insistence as he continued to pack softened Sophie even more. "I'll help him wit' a few things, Ms. Laura. You can go and get some rest for all the traveling."

Laura backed into the hallway. She worried her decision to allow Jessie to join them in Miami was the wrong one. She was easily moved by any show of emotion on his end—it was all any of them had to gauge what he wanted or felt, and sometimes it spoke louder than words. Laura resisted the urge to spoil the boy as she sought opportunities to help him escape his torment. She knew her prayers for breakthrough had been heard, so she exercised patience and believed there would be a turn in Jessie.

As Laura stood in contemplation, a dark figure approached the opening of the walkway. Laura noticed without being alarmed. Allan was sharply dressed in his Universal African Legion uniform; his expression was harsh. Laura had never noticed him stand so tall—so serious. He removed his uniform hat, and stared from a distance.

"When did you arrive?" Laura asked, cold as the fleeting winter. He slowly approached her. She examined his face for a hint of his purpose there.

"I came a little early." The sound of Allan's voice had escaped Laura's memory, but she was reminded. "Wanted to see if there is anything you need." He stopped close enough to reach out and grab her if he desired, and propped himself against the wall.

"Early? I didn't expect you to be here at all." She glanced back into the room where Sophie continued to assist Jessie. "I'm glad you are well," Laura said as she attempted to brush past him, but he tugged slightly at her arm and prevented her.

"Are you sure you want to go back to Miami? Around here, and as far south as Orlando and Tampa, you're speaking nearly every night each week. I've heard of them all." Laura looked down at her arm, which was held steadily, and Allan released her. "Why go back to Miami? I get it— you want to keep your word, but there are people who would rather you stay as far away from the city as possible."

With staggering nonchalance, Laura said, "I'm not moved." Laura tried to end the discussion and walked hastily towards the kitchen, but Allan followed.

"Of course, you're not. Just disregard all the nasty calls and letters, and Garvey loyalists taking over your engagements. None of that is important, right?"

Laura packed sandwiches and slices of cake wrapped in plastic into a small bag on the kitchen table. "No! This— this is important. For each letter and phone call that means harm, I have 1,000 more that favor me." They both searched for what to say. "Must we do this each occasion you disagree? Have you not grown tired yet?"

Allan resisted his initial response, and mustered a "no". He rested his hands against the table while he contemplated a solution that would cause Laura to avoid Miami, and would not further the conflict. Laura stuffed the remainder of the food into the bag. "What can I carry for you?" Allan asked.

"There is a suitcase on my bedroom floor. Sophie is preparing one for Jessie, and she should have her own as well," Laura said.

He pleaded, "Can you stop one moment and think about this?"

"You said, back there, your cause was to come here and offer me help." The more frustrated she became with the man who had been absent for months, the more the sound of Africa amplified in her voice. She panted, "You lied. You've come here to be who you've always been. A man wanting to stop me from what I've been called here to do."

He raised his voice in response, "Stop you? I'm the reason you're connected with these people down here. I know when it's time to call it, and it's time, Laura. Stay here," he commanded.

"That's too bad. You haven't been given a say," she smirked.

Allan stared dotingly upon her, and offered, "The man driving us—I'll pay him a little extra to keep watch. There is no arguing that." He walked away to gather the rest of the belongings, and left Laura, eyes widened and lips parted, alone in the kitchen.

~

The group traveled by train to Miami, and hired a car to more easily access the venues where Laura would speak. Allan sat coolly on its passenger side while Sophie, Laura, and Jessie were seated behind him. As the driver, Quincy, pulled into a fueling station, Laura looked down to Jessie who was seated next to her, and noticed the slight tremble of his leg.

"Need to go now?" she asked, and Jessie nodded. "Allan,

can you take the boy to relieve himself? It's been a while."

"Yeah, I was heading that way myself."

Both, Allan and Quincy exited the car, followed by Jessie. Sophie joined them. "I'm gonna see what kinda' goods they have heah. Would yah like anything?" she offered Laura.

"No. I am fine," Laura responded.

Playfully, Sophie declared, "Well, I'll bring yah somethin' anyway," and she sprang from the vehicle.

Laura sat quietly in the car as her entire entourage helped themselves to a break. The sudden peace was what she needed to gather her thoughts, and to gain a clear sense of direction for the upcoming events. Laura took in her surroundings and pondered the journey ahead until she noticed a man. He walked slowly from the cashier's stand. His face was tense; his brows nearly met. The pink of his bottom lip greatly contrasted with the darkness of his skin. He neared the vehicle close enough to tap the hood if he so dared. He locked eyes with Laura, still inside. Abruptly, he broke his stare and nodded at the driver who waited for the attendant to fuel the car. Laura looked through the window for the driver; he gazed at her.

Startled, Laura whispered, "Take me in the presence of my children that they may be witness that I went down for them." She closed her eyes gracefully in quiet meditation.

Allan nudged at the door and climbed back inside before Jessie and Sophie rejoined Laura in the backseat.

Sophie declared, "I found some good ole oatmeal cookies, Ms. Laura. I gotta extra one heah fuh yah." She extended the cookie over Jessie's small frame, but Laura was distracted by the driver who returned to his seat and adjusted the rearview mirror to place her within his view.

"Thank you." Laura finally accepted and took a small bite of the cookie as she stared at the lurking eyes in the rearview mirror. "We shouldn't be too far from the Alexander house by now."

"No ma'am. Just about 15 miles north of here," the

driver responded.

"Very well. We will all need rest for this evening."

"I'm actually heading off to a meeting at 5, but I'll be sure to join you around 7 before it begins. The meeting's in the same area," Allan announced. "We'll get you all off to the Alexander's." He turned to the driver, "Quincy, if you don't mind, can you take me on to my meeting place?"

"No problem," Quincy agreed.

The group engaged in conversation during the commute—a little about Miami and the improvements needed to create viable communities for blacks, possible steps to acquire adequate educational resources for their children, and what must happen for lasting change. When Sophie's sentimental contributions to the discussion consistently conflicted with Allan's militant suggestions, Laura realized those she cherished most on her journey in America were finally back together again. There were instances where she would simply listen, bask in their voices—from Sophie's occasional squeal to Allan's assertive, guttural tone—and she knew that between them, like each of the voices in black places, they would find solutions to all that plagued them. Discussion represented the start of progress; and the acceptance of differences was the key to unity.

Jessie, far from engaged, dozed off, tucked his head beneath Laura's arm and rested it on her breast.

A hush fell within the car. When all parties were emptied of their relevant insights, Laura looked at Sophie. "When do you believe is his birthday?"

"Whose? Jessie's?"

"It must have passed us in all this time, or it's near."

"Maybe. But the boy never said."

Laura looked down to Jessie. "And he probably won't."

"Yah think we could just give 'em a new one?"

"I never considered, but I don't see why we couldn't."

"Perhaps when we get back tuh Jacksonville. Sure Rachel wouldn't mind herself a little party wit' Jessie."

Sophie smiled. "I'll make sure all the kids around the neighborhood come, and get Allan tuh help out too—soon as we get back and settled."

"I think he'd love that—but it's always hard to tell."

When the group arrived at the Alexander house, the driver ushered Sophie and Jessie inside. Jessie, challenged with the weight of his sleepy head atop his fatigued little body, was lifted into the air and carried by Quincy down the narrow walkway.

Allan lingered for a short while near Laura's car door before he opened it. When the others were completely out sight, he said, "We made it." Allan stepped away for Laura to exit. She stretched, and released a sigh. "Ms. Laura." He backed himself against the car door. "There are some things I've been meaning to tell you." Laura fixed her loosely draped scarf, delicately wrapped about her neck, and listened. "In Connecticut—you meant well—to do something nice for me. I was rude. And you didn't deserve that."

"No need to apologize." She gracefully placed her hand on his shoulder. "There was much taking place, and emotions are difficult to channel when you've been overcome by them."

"No. I don't agree. I could've done better by you." Quincy returned to the car, pulled the travel bags from the trunk, and walked them up to the porch as the two waited for him to pass. "I haven't been good—a good friend to you. And I'm sorry."

"It is well, Allan. I hold nothing in my heart against you." Laura started to walk in the direction of the house, and away from Allan.

"But there is just one more thing," Allan called out as he walked towards her. Laura stopped and turned; and they met face to face.

"Come on, brother. I have a tight schedule," Quincy said with urgency as he passed them. He closed the trunk of the car, sat in the driver's seat and started the engine.

"It can wait until later, I suppose," Allan said in a whisper. "You rest well now. I will see you this evening." He backed up to the car, stepped in and closed the door.

Laura watched the car as it moved further into the distance and wondered what Allan had desired to share.

# CHAPTER
# FIFTEEN

It was as if Laura had never left Miami. Followers she established there the previous year remained loyal, and thirsted for one of her charismatic lectures. They arrived in droves, unapologetic for their stance in her corner, and regardless of all the naysayers and articles intended to part them.

By the third night of her visit, Laura's engagements had successfully drawn thousands into Liberty Hall, and miraculously raised a few thousand dollars. The news of Laura's return did not sit well with UNIA representatives who had once welcomed her—and her ability to acquire new members and raise money. At that juncture, they had both disowned and dishonored her; and once they noticed her success, the scars of their own abandonment had whelped up and was infected with envy.

On the fourth night, confrontation was no longer at

bay, and the rope between Laura and her rival ex-colleagues was shortened. It was like most nights Laura spoke; there was barely room to stand in the auditorium. Nimmo and an accomplice pushed through the crowd to position themselves where Laura could see them clearly. They desired her full attention, but she refused to oblige.

"The message is this: the time is now for each of us to do our share. To have unity, we must first agree. To agree, we must choose to love. To love, we must choose to accept. To accept, we must not count the wrongs of others. We must not compare his convictions or her convictions, or his attitude, or her values, or his shortcomings, or her actions, to our own. We are all equally flawed and perfectly human. Know this: we are all pieces of God's greatly designed, unflawed masterpiece. We need your piece to perfect His plan. The time is now."

James Nimmo waved his arms in the air several times to gain her attention. She noticed but, at once, refused to acknowledge any further.

"Do not be distracted by what others think," she continued to speak. "This journey is for the focused, for those who refuse to relent in their pursuit. To be understood and loved may not always come with what is being required of you to lead your people into a better way. One aligned with the riches of His glory."

"Hey!" Nimmo yelled, and the crowd stirred and noticed the source of the uproar. "You ain't welcomed here," he continued, and Laura could no longer ignore. Two men worked their way through the crowd and attempted to escort him away. "You ain't shit, Laura, and you know it. Deceiving all these good folks and taking their money."

Laura looked out at the audience to gage their position on what had been said. Initially they spoke amongst themselves, whispered and hid their faces from her view, but then the crowd burst into applause. They roared and cheered as the men were removed.

"Keep going, Mother," a voice yelled.

"Never mind them!" came another.

Laura smiled politely and pressed a single finger against her lips. A hush fell on the room, and she continued her message—one that, despite the disruption, had failed to miss a beat.

As Laura stepped away from the podium, Sophie and Allan stood in wait of her. Laura offered hugs and prayer to several attendees as most others exited and left for home. A few remained and continued to chat amongst each other.

"What are your thoughts now, Ms. Laura?" Allan inquired as she finally made her way to them.

"Thoughts? The evening was amazing," she responded.

"You know what I meant. I wasn't in here to see it. Didn't get here until late, but the boys in the back told me all about it. Actually, it might've been a good thing I got here when I did."

"No harm in what happened. You can't blame them for wanting attention. I give none to barking dogs."

"These aren't dogs, Ms. Laura. They're men," Allan attempted to rattle Laura with his words and his sharp gaze. Sophie's eyes widened; in an instant, she realized the depth of Allan's alarm.

"Am I to be afraid?" Laura asked innocently.

"You are to be safe. To have some common sense. To get back on that train and high tail it out of here," he said with controlled aggression. He could no longer repress the urge to chuckle to himself, so he did. "You can't be this stubborn."

"Do not mistake determination for stubbornness, Allan. They are not the same."

Sophie's lips parted to offer a bit of her own insight, but she knew her words would be in opposition to her employer's, so she kept quiet.

"Here we go," Allan said under his breath. "I have Rodney back there," he pointed, "and Jacob over there. If you really want to stay another three nights, we must be sure to keep the hecklers out. It's bad for business."

"It's not *my* business—it's God's business. Let them come if they must. I'll only—." Laura's words were interrupted by the presence of a fourth body within their circle.

"Are you okay, Ms. Laura? I saw the whole thing from over there," Carmen, Allan's old friend, said after she gained the attention of the others. Allan's eyes widened and he stared at her absentmindedly.

"I have no complaints," Laura said. "I see you have been well." Laura extended herself for a hug.

"That's good. It's so good to see you." It was impossible for even a penny to part the women's tight embrace. "You've been missed, Ms. Laura," Carmen whispered. "I wondered how well you would get along in Jacksonville without Allan all this time."

"Well, I've been established quite well, and Sophie is always great help." Laura smiled.

"And great company too, I bet," Carmen giggled.

"Yes, that too," Laura agreed.

"Allan." Carmen nodded in his direction.

"I didn't think you would be coming out this evening, Carmen," Allan said, and clenched his jaw.

"I felt a little better, so I thought I would come out for some air and hear Ms. Laura before she left town."

"You been sick, Ms. Carmen?" Sophie asked.

"A little, but that's to be expected." Carmen chuckled and pat her belly as though it were a small drum.

"A baby?" Sophie gleamed.

"That's what we believe. Everything points to it," Carmen shrugged; her smile no longer appeared crooked, but graceful.

"Oh, what joy and blessings!" Laura smirked. "You're not yet showing. I assume it's really early."

"It's all new." Carmen radiated with energy too difficult to contain. "I'm sure it's a long road ahead for us. Isn't that right, Allan?"

Allan looked at Laura, whose smile quickly diminished. There was a loud thud in the back of the auditorium and each of their heads turned to determine the source.

"Police department!" A white, uniformed officer walked briskly towards the front of the room, followed by eight other officers whose hands held tightly to their batons. They spread themselves throughout the space, and were sure to keep each person in eyesight. "I'll need to see who's in charge here."

The moment was reminiscent of the night in Jacksonville; the one that led Laura to overnight imprisonment; the one she would never hope to experience a second time. "I am," Laura spoke clearly and stepped forward.

The officer approached and courteously addressed the group. "We've received a complaint. And we'll need everyone to exit the building immediately."

"A complaint, sir? Who? What have we done?" Laura inquired.

"You are not the owner of this building. Am I right, ma'am?"

"No, but I have been granted permission to use it for the week."

"Obviously, that is not the case. You may want to take it up with the owners. My job is to address the complaint. I'll need you all to exit."

Some mumbled to themselves, but the sound never elevated above a whisper as each of them gathered their belongings and walked out of the building. Once clear, one officer brought a chain from his automobile, and another officer provided a dense locking mechanism. They chained the door, which made it impossible for anyone to enter. Laura, Sophie, and Jessie watched, bewildered. Allan was no longer there, but the women spotted the driver in the distance. There was nothing left to do but retire for the evening, and they did.

Laura retreated to the bedroom she shared with Jessie

while they stayed at the Alexander house—owned by a wealthy, black doctor and his wife, who were both great supporters of Laura's work. Jessie sat out on the porch and enjoyed a few cookies Mrs. Alexander baked to bribe him into conversation with her. When it still did not come, she assumed it was because his mouth had been filled with sweets.

Sophie, nestled comfortably on the sofa in the family room, listened to the radio as she awaited an answer from Laura—one that would typically come after her time in prayer, and one that she silently hoped would lead them on their way back to Jacksonville.

Unexpectedly, Allan's voice interrupted the sound of jazz. "Hey, is she here?" he spoke quickly.

"She is, but I think she prayin'—been quiet all this time. She ain't been out since we got dropped off either," Sophie offered, but did not turn to look his way.

"I'm sure she's praying," Allan said confidently. "I know this isn't what she planned for."

"Yah think so, huh? How could she prepare fuh somethin' like this?" Sophie reflected. "Poor Ms. Laura." She finally looked at Allan. "She deserved better."

Allan quickly unearthed the root of her comment. "It's not that way, Sophie. You know I wouldn't do anything to—." He sat next to Sophie.

"It's not fuh me tuh heah this. It won't make a bit o' difference tuh me," she said nonchalantly and then walked away. Allan sat there and listened to the sound of trumpets that blared through the stereo as he plotted his next move.

The hallway was dark and quiet. Cold, it led to the back bedroom where Laura was holed up. The floor creaked and broke the peace as Allan's movements made it clear that someone was there. Behind the locked bedroom door, Laura was not in prayer. She had not uttered a word to God all evening, but sat in a chair near the window and listened to silence saturated with her own thoughts.

Allan tapped the door with his knuckle. "Ms. Laura."

He waited for a response. "I don't mean to intrude. I just want to talk to you."

Laura heard, but she did not move, nor did she speak.

"If you're ready—I mean, if you have the peace to go home, I can arrange that for you. You can leave in the morning—*if* you're ready." Still, silence. "If not, remember, I have a few more guys ready to help however they can tomorrow, and the night after if need be."

Laura did not budge, or signal that he had been heard.

"Can you open the door, Ms. Laura? I'd rather not talk this way." He attempted to turn the knob, but the door would not open. He slapped the door with the palm of his hand, and Laura looked towards the source of the sound. Allan placed his forehead against it and his speech became desperate. "I can do what you need me to do, Laura. Just talk to me." He waited, but nothing came. Every emotion he suppressed surfaced, and he wanted to pour out words of endearment he felt unworthy to give. The weight of his guilt caused him to swallow them instead; and they were bitter, and heavy, and stopped dead in his throat. But Laura, graced with discernment, sensed the unsaid from behind the door, and locked it within her soul.

Allan heard footsteps on the creaking floor, so postured himself to walk away as though his business there was done.

"Allan," Dr. Alexander called out.

"Good evening, sir." Allan extended his hand in salutation.

"It's a shame what's taken place," Dr. Alexander said as the men locked hands. "She's been in there since late afternoon." He folded his arms in front of his body. "Sophie told me about it all."

"Looks like it's finally come to an end this go around." Allan sniffled and tried to fully gain his composure; he looked puzzled, as if he could not understand the source of his emotion. "I can send the car to get them all in the morning for the train back to Jacksonville."

"That may not be necessary."

"I'm sure she'd want to get back to Jacksonville as soon as she can—her, Sophie, and Jessie. She can work plenty up there. I'm grateful for you allowing them to stay here, but—."

"It seems she's decided to stay a little longer," Dr. Alexander interrupted.

"Why? How? The venue's been locked up. Police order. There ain't no getting in there now."

"Fox Thomson Hall—not far from Liberty. I know the owners and they're willing to help. They said the place is all hers if she wants it. Seeing how she come in this afternoon, I took it upon myself to make the call."

Allan looked over his shoulder towards Laura's bedroom and then moved closer to Dr. Alexander. "So, Laura knows this?" he asked in a low tone.

"Yes," he said. Dr. Alexander noticed Allan's desire to be discreet, and his apparent disappointment. He said apologetically, "And she's already confirmed, son."

# CHAPTER
# SIXTEEN

## march 8 1928

The cool, evening air ushered in the crowd as the sun set in the distance. And in a back room of Fox Thomson's Hall, Laura prepared to take the podium. She paced the floor and prayed for those who would attend that Thursday evening, and for the words to share with them. On occasion, Laura released a sigh as she pressed forward in prayer, but she refused to allow her own thoughts to disrupt what she was certain God had called her to do. It was no easy feat.

Jessie sat quietly in a corner and playfully kicked his feet to the rhythm of drums that were pounded in the main room.

The door opened suddenly, and Sophie entered. "Anything I can get fuh yah, Ms. Laura?" she asked as she walked over to help Laura with the sleeves of her navy-blue dress.

"Yes, there is." Sophie waited to hear the instructions. "I would like for you to sing this evening."

Sophie did not respond initially, and kneeled to check the hem of Laura's skirt—one she had altered before they left Jacksonville. "Yah never asked me tuh sing befo', Ms. Laura. And I never sang in front of a crowd so big." Sophie stood and shook her head in defiance. "I don't know."

"I want to hear what you sang before. You remember? You sang it so beautifully. God was there. He needs to be here. Sing," Laura pleaded as she cupped Sophie's hands within hers.

"Yes ma'am." Sophie gently removed her hands from Laura's grip and nervously examined Laura's hair, pulled tightly into a bun.

"I'm fine. Go. Sing," Laura said.

Sophie smiled and walked towards the door. "But wait, Ms. Laura. There is one more thing," she added.

"What's that, Sophie?"

"I finally got word from Brewster—well, I called *them* almost every day this week," she chuckled. "They chose me, Ms. Laura. I get tuh start the nursing program soon, and I'm so excited."

Laura became lightheaded, which she attributed to the news she had received, and she smiled. "I knew you could do it. God be praised! My God be praised! I didn't doubt for a moment."

Sophie nodded her head, and she exited, but not before she stopped to look back and flash a smile towards Laura, who maintained a pleasant glow.

Laura walked over to Jessie, gently cupped his chin with her hand, and gave him a slight nod. Unexpectedly, he took her hand from his chin and clasped it. His eyes glistened as he gazed into Laura's. The drums stopped abruptly, and Sophie began to sing from beyond the room.

*When peace like a river,*
*attendeth my way,*
*When sorrows like sea billows roll.*
*Whatever my lot,*

*thou hast taught me to say*
*it is well, it is well, with my soul*
*It is well with my soul*
*It is well, it is well with my soul.*

Laura, still a little stunned at Jessie's subtle gesture, tilted her head in the direction of the door, and then allowed him to escort her out of the room and toward the platform.

Once in the main room, the crowd extended from wall to wall—eyes wide and hopeful. They worshipped an invisible, yet present, God as Sophie continued to sing. They arose as the woman of God took her position behind the podium. The driver, Quincy, who had doubled as her guard, stood in front of the platform on alert. Jessie took a seat in the front row, and after Sophie concluded her song, she sat next to him.

"I have been in this country for 18 months. In that time, I have seen mourning, suffering, and pain. And I have seen celebration, honor, and excitement. One never weighed more than the other—for you are a resilient people. You hope for better, you strive for more, you work for improvement. And tonight, I am here to tell you that God is saying to take your rest. This does not mean to stop working for greater, but to rest in Him. To trust that all is working out—that your peace is not tied to how well or cruelly you may be treated, no matter what doors may be opened or shut, no matter the lack or abundance. In Him is the peace to sustain you. Worry no more."

With much of the crowd seated, it was suspicious when two men stood simultaneously in the center of the room. One man, short in stature, attempted to make his way toward the front.

From a corner of the room, another man yelled, "Imposter! You're a fraud!" and it created a stir amongst the crowd. A few men who stood nearby, shoved him towards an exit.

A second agitator, in a different corner, shouted, "God

be damned! You speak lies! Voodoo princess!"

From some inconspicuous place, Allan appeared. With as much force as he could muster, he swiftly removed the nuisance from the room; three other men carried him completely out into the dark. Allan made haste to the platform to speak with Laura, and the crowd encouraged her with cheers and applause.

Allan panted, "You don't have to keep going. We can stop this now."

Laura bent a little for him to hear her clearly. "No. There is more. I am not finished yet," she said slowly.

"I am right here. You hear me?" Allan said with squinted eyes.

Laura nodded, and he moved away—back into the position he quietly kept until the disturbance. While Allan's back was turned, Laura signaled for the guard who stood in front of the platform to be seated. Quincy was initially puzzled by her command, but she calmly signaled again as she spoke to the crowd, and he complied.

She lifted her voice again as though nothing had occurred. She was poised; her delivery was serene, and the people were wooed into stillness. "Children, hard times are around the corner. You are going to lose your jobs and never get them back. Times will be so hard until you will eat out of garbage cans. You will sign many papers to help your condition, but it will only be for a while."

As Allan slowly walked to the back of the room, he gazed at the crowd and searched it without fail. He noticed James Nimmo, who attempted to blend with the others. Allan looked to Laura, who continued to speak, and tried to make his way to James without a disturbance. On his way, he was surprised by Maxwell Cook's presence; he stood against a wall, and was shielded by a small pillar within a few feet of the podium.

Laura spoke, "Many of you will be glad to work for something to eat. Many will commit suicide, because they will be unable to stand the storms to come. This is what

God has sent me to share. But you must remember, dear children, rest in Him."

Allan watched as James stood and manipulated a bag he carried on his shoulder.

"No. No. No." Allan whispered to himself. He quickened his steps and pressed his way through the crowd while he kept his eyes on Maxwell's movements.

Laura's voice was firm. "Allow Him to be your peace in turmoil. Let not your heart be troubled."

James nodded his head—a signal—and then turned to see Allan within inches of him. Before James could speak, Allan's tight fist made intense contact with James' right eye, and he fell to the floor. A gun shot was heard—and then another. Their origins obscure.

Allan's heart pounded in his ears and throat, and he looked to the podium again, but Laura was no longer there. A scream rang out from the front of the room. Pandemonium. Women escaped with their children; several men were assembled not far from where the princess once stood. Legs and arms flailed violently in the air as the group viciously attacked Maxwell.

Allan fought against the wave of the crowd, and found Laura on the floor. Sophie, already there, kneeled near her and cried out desperately. "God, help us! Please God! Help her!" Sophie screamed.

Allan towered over the two women with severe, in-concealable disgust and pain. A bullet had entered the side of Laura's face, and the once beautiful woman he adored, was disfigured and lifeless.

Allan spoke angrily. "Cover her up! Cover her!"

A woman trembled as she carried over a large cloth. Allan snatched it from her and kneeled under the burden of his grief to place it over Laura's face. He lifted his head and noticed Jessie seated on the front row; he silently wept and stared blankly at the horrific demonstration in front of him. Allan's heart swelled up within him, and he felt he would suffocate.

Allan staggered from the building outraged and overcome with the reality of Laura's demise. The crowd around him moved in and out of focus. He noticed several police cars had arrived, as well as emergency vehicles. Ten men were handcuffed on the pavement; each of them sat as still as possible—shoulders back and eyes straight ahead—to avoid unnecessary police confrontation. James had been arrested as well, but he sat in the backseat of an officer's car. He nervously peered from the window, and witnessed the commotion from behind the safety of the steel door.

The crowd shifted away from the entry, and Maxwell Cook's expired body was carried from the building and placed into an emergency vehicle. There was significant chatter amongst those who stood by.

"They killed him," a man said. "Let's just hope they got the right one."

Allan walked over to the car where James was held until officers could restore order and make sense of all the chaos. Allan gazed fiercely through the window at the cuffed man, his friend. James merely turned his head to look forward.

And soon, Laura's body was carried beyond the walls of the meeting place. The crowd grew silent, but several women wept as they followed the men who carried her. Allan resisted the urge to go near. He sluggishly took a seat on the ground away from the commotion, and watched as the men laid her gently on an ambulance cot; he watched as Sophie attempted to catch her breath between each of her wails, and he watched as Jessie saluted Laura with silence before the ambulance doors were closed.

~

In the empty Jacksonville church a week later, Allan sat in a somber solitude. He expected many to join him for a memorial service in honor of the slain woman, but it would not begin for hours. He was alone in a space where he had spent so little time in previous months; a space built by the hands of a woman he loved dearly, and by those who loved her just as much.

Jessie walked into the sanctuary. He handed the stack of mail he carried over to Allan, and then sat next to him.

"Thank you," Allan said, and slouched in the chair. He slowly sorted through the envelopes. One, postmarked from Africa and addressed to Laura, caught his attention. Also curious, Jessie moved closer to Allan as he opened it. The letter was from King Knesipi, Laura's father. It read:

*Daughter, I believe you are in your rightful place, and doing the Lord's work. It does astonish me that you have taken a liking to a man there. I trust you with my blessing to seek after all your heart desires. Please come home when time permits.*

Allan took a moment to digest the contents of the letter, and the truth behind the king's words. Had Allan been the object of Laura's affection? Either he truly was not certain, or his guilt clouded his ability to receive it.

"If we had never met," Allan said as his lips trembled. "If we had never met, Ms. Laura would still be here, Jessie." And then he buried his face in his hands and wept.

Jessie placed a hand on Allan's shoulder and lightly swept it back and forth. "Do not weep," he spoke. "The enemy has not won. *You* are still here."

Allan quickly wiped his nose with the back of his hand, and looked to Jessie. The boy had finally spoken.

"Is it my birthday?" he asked solemnly.

## about the author

CHRISTINE RACHEAL (ray-shell) WILSON is a published author of four books (*Trickery, Healed Women Don't Cry, Sleeping Adam,* and *Black Gold*) and a screenwriter from Jacksonville, Florida. She attended Douglas Anderson School of the Arts where she studied Creative Writing, and is a graduate of Florida State University, where she received a Bachelor of Arts in English-Creative Writing and Business Management. Christine is the founding owner of Airris Books and Media, a consulting firm that helps new authors to achieve their publishing goals. She is also a co-owner of the media company Opal Ally, and the mind behind the Melanated Lit Podcast. (*www.melanatedlit.com*) She resides in Atlanta, Georgia with her husband, Larry, and their two children.

For more information, visit
**www.christineracheal.com**